REG

REG

By

RICK GROVES

In Memory of Susan

CHAPTER 1

Reginald was very distraught. The reason? You may well ask. I say again, you may well ask. Lordy, Lordy, Lordy, YOU MAY WELL ASK!

Well, to be quite honest, nobody really knew. Nobody really knew for the first time in three weeks or maybe four, depending on your own concept of time.

You will understand that I'm typing this from memory and I'm not exactly the world's most brilliant typist, as you can see by the cock-ups in this sentence. Incidentally, my memory isn t so hot, either.

Anyway, I digress. As I was saying, or should I say, TYPING, Reginald suddenly became distraught. The reason? Ah, the reason.

Reginald, or Our Reg as he was known by his family and friends—or should I say, friend. Come to think of it, he didn't have any family either, as they were all dead. Except maybe you could count his cousin Regina, but she has been in a lunatic asylum since she was 12, or so Reg tells me. So that leaves me, Reg's friend. Being a friend of Reg's this left me Privy to Certain Types of Informat on About Reg—if you know what I mean—for what it was worth.

Reg was an extremely secretive fellow, so secretive in fact that sometimes he didn't know when he'd last had aba th—sorry, that should read, a bath. The reason he didn't know was because he was so secretive that he would keep bath night a secret from himself! This he divulged to me in the strictest confidence one day when I remarked on the slight pong in his living-room. Anyway, on this particular day, when I called on Reg, I could see he was in an extremely agitated state, he was pacing up and down the living-room floor—well it wouldn't be the ceiling, would it?

As he was getting on my nerves a bit I said, "What's up, Reg?"

"I'm not telling you, it's a secret," was his reply.

I knew all I had to do was wait, because Reg was a secretive sort of person, but he wasn't very good at keeping secrets—know what ah mean man? So I just shrugged my shoulders and said, "OK, suit yourself," and sat down on his moth-eaten sofa.

About five minutes of pacing up and down followed.

"Can you keep a secret?" said Reg.

"Sure I can, it's the other buggers that can't," I replied.

Reg wrung his hands. Five more minutes of pacing, "It's Albert," he said.

"Albert. Albert, who? I asked, puzzled.

You know, THE Albert," said Reg in a sort of furtive way from behind his hand.

I was getting a bit annoyed by now. "Look, Reg," I retorted. "There must be thousands of bloody Albert's, Albert who? For God's sake?"

"Albert Einstein," he replied, looking distraught.

"Oh, THAT Albert," I said, "He was only one of the greatest mathematicians and theoretical physicists that ever lived, if not the greatest. We owe our concept of the physical world from the microcosm to the macrocosm to him." (You can see that I knew exactly which Albert Reg was on about.) "What's it to do with you, he's been dead for years."

"What's it got to do with me? WHAT'S it got to do with me?" Reg practically yelled. "I'll tell you what it's got to do with me, I'm bloody well disillusioned with him that's what."

I could see that Reg was well dis-TRAUGHT. "Look Reg," I said in a friendly conspiratorial sort of way, "Why don't you pour us both a Jack Daniels and tell me what's bothering you about Albert Einstein, although I can't see what a rotting corpse could do to upset you so much."

Reg went to his cupboard and took out his bottle of that well-known American tipple, Jack Daniels. I licked my lips expectantly. Reg poured two glasses, sank one straight off and kept the other clenched in his tight-fisted fist. He sat down opposite me.

"Well I'm disillusioned with him on two counts, really."

"OK, Reg, hit me with number one," I said, glaring at him.

"Right, I will," said Reg, sipping the other Jack Daniels. "I always thought that Albert Einstein, Albert bloody Einstein was a great big macho man with a 42-inch chest and carried a flippin' great machine-gun with a bandeleiro of bullets around him and a killer knife in his belt. I thought he went around killing and beating everybody up because he was a slightly mixed-up ex-Vietnam veteran."

Reg almost sobbed, "I thought he was a brilliant body-builder, a struggling prize-fighter. But no, what do I find. What do I FIND, I picked up a copy of The Guardian this morning, turned to the children's page and there, complete with his photograph is an article on this so-called Einstein. Instead of a set of 20-inch biceps and a pair of tight-fitting ex-marine's trousers is this doddering old codger with grey hair and a stupid moustache. And to cap it all, the heaviest thing he's ever lifted is a sodding pencil! And he got his bus fare wrong when he was going to the shops! All he ever did was write down bloody sums on the backs of envelopes.

"It's annoying me greatly. I suppose that's why you could say I'm extremely disillusioned."

"But Reg, you can't blame Einstein for the fact that you got him mixed up with Sylvester Stallone, can you?" I said. I was getting a bit parched by now, "Have you got anything for me to drink?" I queried.

"Oh sure," said Reg absentmindedly. He picked up the two glasses and poured himself another Jack Daniels. He then went over to the tap and filled the other with water and offered it to me. "There you go, I didn't know you were thirsty."

I glared at Reg and took—or should I say swiped—the glass from his hand.

"What was I saying about getting Einstein mixed up with this bloke Victor Sylvester or whoever."

"Victor Sylvester was a dance band leader Reg," I replied. "He used to be on Come Dancing. However, as I was saying, you can't blame him because you got him mixed up."

"Who? Sylvester Stallone, Victor Sylvester or Einstein?" Reg said.

"Einstein," I sighed.

"Oh, Einstein. No, no bugger that, I don't mean that I'm disillusioned with him because he's not got bulging biceps or anything like that. It's the other thing . . ."

"What other thing, Reg?"

I took a reluctant swig of water. Reg sipped his Jack Daniels.

"That crackpot theory of his."

I choked on my water, "CRACKPOT!"

Reg slapped me on my back, "Are you OK? I'll get you something stronger."

"Ooh, ta," I said triumphantly.

Reg poured two glasses of Jack Daniels, drank one, and sat down with the other in his hand.

I held my head in my hands. I was getting just a bit fed up with Reg.

"Where were we?" said Reg, taking a sip.

I was beginning to wonder just how absentminded Reg was, the crafty bastard.

I looked round Reg's room, at the threadbare carpet, his knackered three-piece, his old pre-war sideboard, the contemporary wallpaper complete with plastic ducks in full flight on the wall.

This is the man who dares to call Einstein's theory crackpot, I thought.

"We are talking about the Theory of Relativity aren't we, Reg," I said.

"Course we are, stupid," he retorted.

"Naturally," I sighed. I wondered to myself what training had Reg had to challenge one of the world's greatest mathematicians? What had Reg ever had to offer the human race in the form of art, science, music, etc. Had he ever designed a great cathedral? Maybe had a hand in the invention of the computer, put man on the moon, swum the channel? Or one length of the local baths even? Had he been taking an Open University course in secret?

"Have you been taking an Open University course in secret, Reg?" I queried.

"No, I've been too busy for that."

Too busy—I thought back over the last few months. I thought of the mornings when I had knocked on his door when he was fast asleep in bed—of the afternoons when I had knocked on his door when he was fast asleep in bed. The busiest I had ever seen Reg was when he was eating his chips in front of the telly, while watching Blue Peter or Brookside. Mind you, he has been known to break into a fast walk when going down to the post office for his money. No, I could honestly say that Reg was definitely having me on, there.

"You've never been busy in your life Reg," I glared.

"Well I was yesterday," he replied.

"Oh yes, doing what?"

"Reading?"

"Oh, reading, that is being busy Reg. What was it, War and Peace? The complete works of Willie Shakespeare? All the volumes of The Encyclopedia Britanrica? Or maybe it was 1001 Arabian bloody Nights," I felt a faint urge to strike Reg in between the eyes.

"You can be busily reading, you know, and that—he leaned forward—is why I know for a fact that Einstein got it all wrong."

7

I couldn't help it—I started laughing my socks off. After a few minutes, and with tears still rolling down my face I said, "Are you really saying that Al Einstein got his own theory cocked up? Look Reg, you aren't qualified to tell if Terry Wogan has got his facts right when he's doing an interview, let alone Albert Einstein's relativistic equations!"

"Albert Einstein's relativistic whats?" said Reg.

"Oh, never mind."

Reg looked at me in a hurt, puckered sort of way, "I'll have you know that I have been doing a bit of reading on the subject."

"Oh yeah, like what, for instance?"

"Well, it was called The Young Man's Guide to Relativity."

"I can't say I've ever heard of that one, Reg."

"Well it was called The Toddler's Guide actually."

I must admit I giggled a bit more.

Reg glared—"Well, it told it like it is, no nonsense, without all those bloody sums!"

"Yes, OK, but don't you think all those bloody sums—as you put it—might have been necessary?"

"That's just it! If you've cocked it up at the very start, then there's no need for bloody sodding sums!"

I think Reg was getting a bit annoyed with me now.

"Alright then Reg, which bit was cocked up?"

"I don't feel that I want to tell you after all."

I could see that it was time to humor Reg.—"Whose turn is it for the Indian takeaway?"

Quick as a flash—"Yours."

"Are you sure I didn't get it last time?"

"Yours."

"Very well, what do you fancy?"

"A vindaloo with a Bangalore Torpedo on the side."

CHAPTER 2

I slipped out of Reg's house with a smile on my face even though Reg had never ever bought a takeaway as long as I had known him. Never mind, I was beginning to enjoy myself. It was just turning eight p.m. I decided I would get a beef Rogan Josh and—sod it—a couple of four packs.

I thought I'd try the Indian that was near the newly modernized yuppie flats. They had just advertised by bill-posting all the local houses. I jumped into my new Metro Quest and set off.

I was quite pleased with my new car but was still missing my Renault 19 that I had just part exchanged. The bastards had only given me three grand for it, and there it was on the forecourt the very next day for £4195. And to cap it all, it looked as if it had been sold the day after that.

I reached out to put on my Mike Oldfield tape—all that talk about Relativity had made me come over all philosophical—I forgot—I hadn't had a radio cassette fitted. If this had have been a Renault it would have had one as standard—bastards.

Oh shit, I had nearly missed the takeaway!

I pulled up and popped on the alarm that they had charged me extra for—and went into the shop. A rather surprised Indian gentleman looked up from behind the counter.

"Yes."

"Can you do me a couple of takeaways please?"

"Well, we'll see what we can do."

The shop had previously been owned by a bloke called Nigel who had had it as a restaurant and called it Jester's. He reckoned it would go a bomb with all the young trendies in the new flats opposite. It bombed all right—he ended up turning it into a transport caff and then sandwich bar—it just never caught on. Then he must have sold it to this lot.

"Right, I'll have a beef Rogan Josh and a Vindaloo with a Bangalore Torpedo on the side."

"What was that on the side?"

"A Bangalore Torpedo."

"Are you taking the piss, mate?" I noticed that three other Indians were sitting at the dimly-lit corner table, playing cards. They looked up in unison.

Not that I know of."

His face split into a huge grin as he said "I think you had better look up Bangalore Torpedo in your encyclopedia when you get back." The three gentlemen in the corner carried on with their card game.

Phew, I'll kill reg when I get back.

"I'll knock you something up in a jiff" said my Indian friend, "Was it for two?"

"Yes, it is mate."

"Ahh, romantica, eh?"

"Oh, no," how could I tell him that I was having a night in with Reg discussing Albert Einstein?

He just looked at me and went into the back. One of the blokes in the corner shook his head and dealt another hand.

As I was waiting for whatever it was that was cooking, I had a look round the place. It didn't look as though it had seen a cleaning lady since Nigel had left it. The floor was still carpeted and it was decidedly sticky underfoot. The tables were like the counter—Yuk! There were no other customers.

15 minutes later I was still waiting. Putting my hands in my pockets—like you do when you're getting a bit cheesed off—I found the billpost that they had shoved through the letter box. There was quite an impressive list of Indian dishes on it. It didn't seem to live up to it's own advert this place didn't. Shit! I was in the wrong takeaway! I should have gone to the one on Liverpool Street which was near where I lived!

I was just thinking of doing a runner when my Indian pal came out of the back with two steaming plastic trays of whatever it was he had 'knocked up'—it smelt delicious.

"How much is that, pal?"

"Eighteen pounds."

"Are you sure that's how much it is?" I felt a bit apprehensive. The lads in the corner were taking an interest again. There were still no other customers.

He grinned again as he was wrapping up the meals, "Only kidding, that'll be four fifty to you."

This bloke had a funny sense of humor. I wish I'd have gone to the right place.

Ah, good, I had four pounds fifty in my small change. I handed it over and turned to go.

"Tarra cock" he shouted (that's Lancashire for goodbye sir).

See you." I stepped out into the cool night air. Was I glad to be out of there. Just the two four packs to get now, I was starving.

The door of the takeaway burst open. I turned round to see the Indian's head pop out.

"I'f I'd have cooked that at the speed of light you'd have got it 13 minutes ago!"

What a strange thing to say—but he was right.

It was getting on for 8:30 now.

13

I jumped into my trusty Metro and shot off down the road to take a right for Langworthy Road. Just as I was going for the right-hand turn my windscreen was filled with the blaze of lights from an oncoming Ford Fiesta doing about ninety miles an hour. The thing fairly leapt out at me as I swerved to avoid it. I managed to get into a vacant space on my left. My engine stalled as the Fiesta blazed on down the road. I just caught sight of two grinning apes on the back seat. The two Indian takeaways had slipped off the seat onto the floor.

I was shaking a bit—"Bastard retards" I said to myself. "If I had a hammer right now I'd smash their shit-for-brains heads in. I bet they don't even know that Albert Einstein even existed let alone had a theory or two."

Still muttering to myself I picked up the takeaways and restarted the engine. I carried on at a slightly more careful pace.

Next stop, Threshers.

There were a few kids outside the wine store larking about and trying to get the two girls inside the store wound up. I was still a bit annoyed about the near miss in the car, so I picked on the smallest lad and elbowed him in the side of the head.

"Ouch," he yelped, "that hurt."

"Oh, sorry," I cooed, "I didn't see you there." I went into the shop.

The girls were talking about their impending holidays. One was going to Ibiza and the other to Majorca.

"It's great in Majorca but I prefer Ibiza myself, I'm off to Turkey in the next few weeks." I said with a bit of a fixed grin—as I was still as mad as hell inside.

The girls just looked at me as if to say, "We've got one of those been-everywhere buggers here."

I bought two four-packs of Boddies bitter and left after a short chat about the rights and wrongs of sunbathing.

The kids were still outside and the littlest was still rubbing his head. The biggest of them came up to me, "I saw you do that on purpose." He said, "we're under-age you know, and nobody can touch us or put us in prison or any fing like that."

He was wearing a baseball cap back to front. I hate baseball caps, especially when worn back to front.

Sometimes I like to wear my hiking boots and I had them on now.

I pushed my face into his. "Listen you little t**t, I've just been nearly killed by one of your future retarded generation and the mood I'm in now, I'll poke your f**king eyes out and stuff them up your arse, let alone touch you. There's just one thing you should get through that Nintendo-filled cardboard box you call a skull and that is when us decent law-abiding citizens get pushed that bit too far we descend to your f**king level and WE WANT BLOOD." I was shouting by now. Just to get the point home I kicked him on the shin as hard as I could. It was a bit over the top really because I think he had got the point around about poking his eyes out.

I had to sit in the car for a few minutes as I was shaking a bit. I looked over to the kids, the big lad was on the floor hugging his leg, I felt a slight pang of remorse and thought about getting out and saying sorry. Quickly I looked at the four-packs and felt a little more relaxed. "Just get them down you and the world will be a better place." I really must stop talking to myself.

The police helicopter was starting a full circle in the sky directly above me . . . Just another Saturday night on Langworthy Road. My God haven't we progressed since my wife and I had our wedding reception in the Langworthy Hotel opposite? That was 26 years ago, and the place was one of the best in the area with a landlord who always wore a suit and tie. I was looking at the Langworthy now, it was boarded up as a result of an arson attack by the local retards. Something to do with protection money.

I looked up just as the kids were approaching the car. I got the engine started and pulled away just in time to various shouts of abuse from the little cherubs. I thought for a moment of circling the block and running a few of them over—what was I thinking of? The car was virtually brand new! Maybe I'll get them when it's ready for changing. I was chuckling by the time I pulled up outside Reg's red-brick terrace.

Reg always left the door open for me when I went out to get us some supper, so I let myself in. Reg was glued to the telly watching Bruce Forsyth's Generation Game.

"You wouldn't believe the lumber I've just been in, Reg."

"I love watching Brucie."

Goddammit I could have been Jack The Ripper for all he cared.

I got the hint and went into the kitchen to prepare the supper. Reg still had one of those 1950's 'kitchen units', it was olive green with a base part and an upper part which comprised of a cupboard, the bottom part had a drop-leaf work top and two cutlery draws. There were tiny circular air vents on each cupboard door. Reg kept all his worldly kitchen goods in here. I knew it well, I had got many a supper ready at this unit and every time I looked at it I always felt a touch of nostalgia—I was feeling a touch too nostalgic tonight.

First thing—get the beer open—I cracked open the Boddie's can and sank half of it, it was delicious. The only thing was, it was one of those new-fangled draught ones and it wouldn't stop foaming, I had to grab a pint glass quick and pour the rest. I poured another can and took it in to Reg. He was still engrossed in watching Bruce making a fool of this woman in her 50's—Bruce was trying to get her to tap dance and do a rendition of one of Shirley Temple's old numbers, something about a good ship and a lollipop. I shoved the pint into his hand. "Ta," he said, without looking up.

17

"I could still be Jack The Ripper," I thought as I went back to the kitchen and finished off the first can. "Now then, what have we here?" I unwrapped the first takeaway, at least it was still hot. It was made up of large chunks of beef with pieces of pineapple, mushrooms, onions and pilau rice all covered in a hot curry sauce, also there appeared to be a couple of pieces of wood in it!

I rooted in the drawer of the unit and took out one of Reg's many old forks. "Well, here goes." It was delicious, the second meal was exactly the same, a sort of meaty Chum dog food with curry, I bunged them both on plates and took them in.

It was obvious that Reg was not going to discuss Einstein while his beloved Bruce was on the box, anyway the show was due to end in a few minutes. After being given his plate of food, Reg looked, sniffed and looked again.

"What's this? Where's my Bangalore Torpedo? What are these bits of Waney lap fencing doing in my curry?"

"It's a curry from the Indian's that used to be Jester's—I'm going to look up Bangalore Torpedo in the encyclopedia—and that's not Waney lap, it's probably sandlewood—and just get it eaten Reg." I sighed, sinking some more beer.

"OK, I'm only asking, ooh, it's not bad is it?"

We always had this ritual every time we had a takeaway. At last—Bruce was waving a cheerful goodbye to the audience.

Reg was tucking in now, "Meat's a bit chunky isn't it? Just like you get in a tin of dog food."

I got up and picked the Pear's Cyclopedia off Reg's bookshelf and looked up Bangalore Torpedo. "Do you know what a Bangalore Torpedo is, Reg?"

"It's a sausage."

"Cobblers, it's a type of explosive in the form of a drain pipe that they used in the Second World War, come to think of it, John Wayne used one in that film, The Longest Day, and you had me asking for one in the local curry shop, you prat!"

"Sorry," said Reg sheepishly, "Bloody good scoff though old boy, where did you get it from again?"

I told Reg how I had gone into the wrong takeaway shop and what it was like.

"Bloody hell," he replied "You didn't go there did you? That's no curry parlour, the whole things a front for the local hashish mob! It's a wonder you didn't get a knuckle sandwich, never mind a curry!"

Reg started laughing, and we ended up eating our meal like a couple of schoolboys—giggling all the way through it. We were both on our third beer by the time we had finished.

I cleared up, cracked open the two last cans and realised that, yet again, I had waited on Reg hand and foot while he had done sod all as usual.

I offered Reg his last can as he was studying one of the pieces of wood from his meal, "Bloody rum thing to put in a curry," he said, testing it in between his teeth, "Does taste a bit spicy though. Tell you what, I feel a bit pissed, in fact a bit more pister than usual," he giggled, swaying in his chair.

I definitely could feel the beer taking hold, too. It wasn't like me to get sozzled on three cans—better have another drink.

"Well, what about Mr. Einstein then?" I chuckled. (What was so funny about Albert Einstein?)

"Ooooh right," Reg said grinning like a Cheshire cat, "Well, yes, as I was saying, I was reading about him in the paper . . . ." Reg's voice tailed off into the distance as my eyelids creaked to a close and I slumped into the chair, letting the last few drops of Boddie's Best Bitter (brewed in the North) dribble onto his tatty carpet.

I awoke, but my eyes were still closed. It'd been a long time since I had fallen asleep like that. I realised I should be at home by now, tucked up in bed next to my beloved, but for some reason I didn't seem to be too worried about that. I forced my eyes open, Reg was nowhere to be seen. I looked at the clock—it was six in the morning.

As I became more awake I realised I was feeling good—very good. For some reason I had on Army fatigues. I decided I would go out for a walk. In the hall or lobby as Reg called it, was my jacket—an Army combat jacket. I slipped it on, in the pockets were gloves—everything was a perfect fit. I fastened up the jacket, slipped on the gloves and opened

Reg's front door. The street were Reg lived was still cobbled, red-brick terraces ran down one side and the wall of the local bus station ran down the other side. The pavement was still the old pre-war type of stone flags—on the wall of the bus depot were the shrapnel scars of a near miss by a Second World War bomb.

I quietly closed Reg's front door. The air was freezing and it was just starting to become light as I started to walk down the street. The boots on my feet felt great, as though I could walk a thousand miles without any bother. As I continued walking I became aware that I had been joined by a companion, although I couldn't see h s face as it was hidden behind a black ski mask. For some reason I didn't think to question why he was there, it just felt right. We both walked down the street together—by now I was feeling positively elated, every muscle felt like steel springs. I felt as though I should be going in that direction and that I had a purpose, just like I feel when I am fell walking.

As we progressed to the top of the street the terraces came to an end and the side of the pavement began to give way to a slight hollow, there was a sign of frost now. It was nearly full light without a cloud in the sky. We walked on. As I looked down there was about two inches of snow underfoot—the hollow at our side had begun to get steeper with a ten-foot drop and the snow down there looked a bit thicker. As we walked I could feel that I was becoming fitter and everything was standing out clear and sharp like I had never seen it before.

We walked on for another 30 minutes. By now the hollow had given way to a beautiful snow lined valley with mountains

21

outlined against the blue sky, but we were still walking on the pavement. I couldn't feel the cold one bit, I was immune to all that.

The valley dropped away beneath us by at least a thousand feet and we could make out a series of trails running down to the bottom. About a mile along the base of the valley was a small pub nestled into the great drifts of snow.

"I'm gasping for a drink," said my unseen companion.

"So am I," I replied. "But the pub's at least a mile away and more than a thousand feet down. And besides, we'll have to leave the pavement!"

"Don't worry about that—just go for it, you'll be glad you did."

I noticed the start of a trail leading downwards into the valley, it was no different from the mountain trails when I have been fell-walking. (Except for the fact that it was about two feet deep in snow and ice.) Without hesitation I leapt from the pavement and started off at a fast jog downwards, crashing through the snow. I was having the time of my life. For the first time I noticed I was carrying an Armalite rifle. We were both hurling ourselves down the side of the valley and ripping through the snow like hot knives through butter. The pub was getting nearer as the helicopter started to swoop down the valley.

It looked like a wedding reception of very drunk people coming out of the front doorway. "Looks like a bunch of accountants to me," said my companion, "They always behave like this when they are let out on the loose."

The whole group of about twenty people were laughing hysterically and waving bottles of champagne about. We realised that they must know the pilot of the helicopter as they beckoned him to come lower. The idiot started to do it, too!

The helicopter swooped down to about five feet and started to hover over an icy stream—the party of people ran and staggered towards it. My partner and I came to a screeching halt, finding ourselves in the middle of the group

The bride was looking very glamorous in her long white wedding dress. To my horror, one of the drunken trendies launched himself onto one of the helicopter's skis. Seeing this, another two decided to do the same, causing the helicopter to sway and yaw, the pilot was trying desperately to gain control.

With a grating crunch the helicopter hit the deck with its rotors still fanning around digging great chunks out of the snow and ice. This caused it to skid across directly toward the bride who was frozen to the spot in horror. "Do something, damn you!" screamed my companion. "You're always pissing and dithering about!" He grabbed my rifle off me and gave me a shove forward.

"I'll bleedin' show you!" I yelled back.

The helicopter was nearly on its side by now and the rotors were hissing round to within inches of her face. I found myself leaping on to the nose of the 'copter. I could feel the huge draft from the rotors tearing at my combat fatigues. I leapt down onto the ground and planted my feet firmly, took a big breath and grabbed one of the rotors—to my amazement they jammed and I wrestled the whole machine to a standstill!

Still grasping the rotors I took stock of the situation, everybody was standing as still as statues with three Hooray Henrys still flat on the snow. I looked down at the bride, "Ta ever so much," she purred, "Whatever can I do to repay you?" She raised her veil—I was looking into a pair of deep blue eyes and a face that looked oh so familiar. CHRIST, it was Marilyn Monroe!

"Look out," cried Marilyn.

I turned to see my companion standing above me, his teeth bared in a wide grin through the cut-out of his ski mask. He had my rifle raised above his head, butt downwards—he brought it crashing downwards on my head. Everything went black and I began to feel cold

CHAPTER 3

My eyes creaked open once more. There was the same grin—I raised my arms instinctively to protect myself. "Wakey, wakey old pal!" said Reg, grinning down at me, "It's gone half eleven you dozy bugger."

"Where am I?" I croaked.

"In my armchair at number 33," Reg replied, "You're missus is gonna kill you if you don't get going!"

"Reg, you'll never guess the dream I've just had, it was incredible."

"You're going to be incredibly sorry if you don't get off home."

I pulled myself up from his armchair, I wasn't feeling so good now, I was cold and my head was aching. And besides, my leg was asleep. As I creaked across the room to get my coat from the hanger on the back of the door I stubbed my shin on Reg's coffee table. Yes, I definitely wasn't the same person as I was in my dream. "Goodnight Reg," I mumbled as I opened his front door.

"Goodnight mate, you'll have to tell me about your dream the next time you come."

"And you'll have to tell me about Al Einstein." I whispered to myself.

As I stepped out into the frozen night air I couldn't help but look up at the bus depot wall, yes there was the shrapnel marks the same as they have always been. Being over the limit I decided to leave the Metro and walk home. Walking down the street I kept my head down and looked at the pavement. I still couldn't help but feel exhilarated by my dream, and also a little disappointed to be back to the real me. What the hell was it all about? God, it was nearly Sunday morning! I quickened my pace to bring me home to my cozy little semi-detached.

I quietly opened the door to find my wife Prue standing in the hallway.

"Where have you been til now?" she said quietly but firmly.

"I fell asleep at Reg's for some reason—I had this unbelievable dr—."

"You make me sick, if you're not playing with the daft drum machine or warbling on your mouth organ you're round there at that idle sods."

"I don't play WITH it—I try to play it." I must admit that it must sound bloody awful, but it keeps me happy.

"Right, that's it, we're off out tomorrow or else. Just me and you, right?"

"Yes dear."

"Do you want a drink?"

Yesss! I knew things were alright when Prue offered me a drink. "I'll have a whiskey and tonic love," I said with a smile.

I settled in my armchair as Prue came in with the drinks. "You must have fallen into a deep sleep to start dreaming," she said.

"I know, I don't know why—do you want me to tell you about it?"

"Go on then," said Prue looking at me coldly.

"Well, it started in Reg's and I was walking down the street when . . . ."

About half way through my diatribe, Prue interrupted, "this is a bloody long dream Dick, get on with it, it's nearly bed-time!"

Prue was obviously bored so I gave her the abridged version—it just shows you that what you think is exciting is just yawn-making to someone else.

I came to a halt with the rifle butt crashing down on my bonce. "That sounds more like a bloody drug trip than a dream to me," said Prue. "Are you sure you were only drinking beer round there?"

"Course I was," I retorted with all the conviction of being absolutely right.

"Anyway, I'm off to bed."

I could tell Prue was still a bit annoyed with me, so I dug our cat—DJ—out of her sleeping basket and put her gently in her cozy box in the garage, she gave a massive yawn and settled down. I thought how long we had owned her—15 years. Where had that time gone? Did it seem like 15 years to her? I gave her one last stroke under her chin and locked up and went off to bed.

Prue was already in, and it didn't take me long to snuggle up to her soft bum with my arms around her—my favourite place. I went out like a light as usual, thinking about my dream and wondering what Reg was on about, I made a mental note to revise a bit on the Theory of Relativity.

Sunday morning dawned crystal clear and crisp, I could feel a long walk coming on.

Turning to Prue I said "How about getting the boots on, love?"

This was our code for serious walking. Prue yawned and was keen to go when she saw the weather.

I had been looking at my Ordinance Survey map of the Snowdonia area of Wales and had spotted a place called Penmachno just outside Betsy Coed, so we decided to ramble around there. After a flurry of activity—filling up the vacuum flask, making sandwiches, packing the rucksack etc., we were off in our trusty little Metro, listening to 'Talk Radio' on the way. Reg's curtains were all shut, of course. There was a phone-in about some scumbag that had broken into someone's house and had been clobbered by the owner. The owner had been arrested by the police and the listeners were going berserk about the injustice of it. The signal kept on fading because we were listening on our little portable radio.

We made Betsy in about two and a half hours and turned into the B road for Penmachno for about 11 in the morning. The day was as clear as crystal with the mountains and foreground scenery standing out in sharp relief. We decided to park up at the working wool mill about three miles from our destination. We got our boots on and I slung the rucksack onto my back. This was always the best bit, setting off.

I couldn't help but think about my dream, there I was striding along, feeling good and Prue was my unseen companion. I could remember every detail of it, I hadn't lost a single moment There was something in there trying to tell me about myself, I have always been a ditherer but my companion was so decisive, getting annoyed with me for not taking action promptly in fact getting so annoyed that he bopped me on the bonce with his rifle butt.

I can always tell when Prue is enjoying a ramble, she can't stop talking, but I loved her for it, even though we have been married for 28 years we could still talk to each other.

We had been walking along the roadside for about two and a half miles with the hills on either side of us and a stream with the odd waterfall on our right. Prue stopped talking, then after a few minutes said, "It's very quiet, isn't it?"

"It usually is in places like this," I replied.

"I know that, you prat, I mean it really is quiet."

29

I listened to the sound of absolutely nothing. Great. But it was quiet, even the birds had taken a day off. By now the village was coming into view, first we passed a curious tailor's shop which was nothing more than a large wooden shed with a panoramic window at one end and an asphalt roof, several half-finished gents suits hung in the window and you could see the owner's workbench complete with Singer sewing machine (treadle, of course).

I was just thinking what amount of business a tailor could do in a tiny remote village such as this, when we came up to a row of derelict terraced houses with what was left of their slate roofs sagging into the bedrooms. They ran off at an odd angle to the main road and had no backyards but each had its own slate toilet outside and one had the remains of and old tin bath near the backdoor.

"Miner's cottages," I said, "You can just see them having a bath at the back of the house and sitting in those loos reading 'The Pigeon Fancier's Gazette' or something like that."

"You're right, I can picture them," said Prue "I can picture them quite clearly."

I didn't take much notice of her remark as I was too busy getting the cottages into the focus of my camera.

After another row of cottages came another ramshackle wooden building which looked exactly like the trading posts you got in the Canadian Rockies when Davy Crockett was knocking about. It even had a drop-down front for serving customers. I took another photograph. The place was fascinating me no end.

We set off walking again and came up to a small double-bayed bungalow with a 'for sale' sign in its front garden. Without speaking we both went through the garden gate, up the four steps to the front door. I peered through the letterbox, "What can you see?" Prue chattered.

It was a small hallway with a door to the right and one to the left, and then the same again further back, the floor was perfect parquet flooring—the original distemper was still on the walls which I estimated to be about 90 years old. A small skylight threw a pool of sunlight into the hall. At the far end was the unmistakable outline of a grandfather clock. "God, look at this," I said moving to one side to let Prue take a look.

"That looks strange," she said, eyes riveted to the letterbox.

By now I was peering through the bay to the right and into the lounge, it was more of the same—the walls were painted in the original mustard colored distemper, and there was the outline of a sideboard on the wall, a perfect walnut carved fireplace dominated the room. Looking through the left hand window which had probably been the bedroom was a smaller fireplace with the old parquet style oilcloth on the floor, covered by a square of the most threadbare carpet I have ever seen. All the skirting and door frames were walnut varnished. The outside window sills were made of solid slate about three inches thick. "They got there moneys-worth out of that carpet," I said to Prue.

"No, HE got his moneys-worth," she replied.

I looked at her and could see that her pupils had dilated, making her usual blue-green eyes look dark. She was staring straight into the lounge.

"What's up?"

"I'm not too keen about this place, I'm going over the road to sit on the wall." Prue said already going down the front steps.

Frowning, I replied OK, I'll be with you in a mo," I went round the side and took a look into the back garden, which stretched down to a lovely stream. At the back was an old chemical toilet and a mangle for squeezing wet clothes, it looked as if it still worked, too. Coming back to the front I couldn't help take another look at the outline of the grandfather clock at the back of the hallway Holding open the letterbox I set the camera to 'flash' and focused on the outline, I took the photograph—as the flash went off I distinctly saw hands on the clock face saying one O'clock! The front door of the bungalow swung open leaving me staring at the outline in the hall in a semi-crouched position. I straightened up and walked into the hall, there was plenty of light, it was just an outline—no hands—no face. I backed out and down the steps and across the road to Prue. "You'll never believe this!" I gasped.

"What time is it?" her pupils were enormous.

'One o'clock' I replied.

"Come on, let's go." I said taking hold of Prue's arm and directing her on through the village.

We walked on for about two minutes not really seeing any of our surroundings, we were both deep in thought. "You go first," I said.

"What do you mean 'go first'," she answered.

"You know, tell me what you saw—then I'll tell you what I saw."

"Let's stop somewhere for a bite to eat, then we can talk."

We carried on for about another five minutes and saw a small pub on the right. "We'll stop there and get a drink."

The weather was lovely so Prue got settled at a small cast-iron table at the front of the pub. I went in and ordered a half of bitter for me and a diet Coke for her. The pub was tiny and tatty and the bar was no bigger than our kitchen worktop at home, the main and only room was 'L' shaped with a large fireplace at the bottom of the 'L', around it were sat half a dozen locals. The fireplace was black with a slate surround, it must have been about nine feet high up to the mantle shelf over which there was an inscription in Welsh. The landlord put the half bitter in front of me, "Take a mouthful," he said. Dutifully I did so, "Take another, we don't give a toss here," smiled the landlord. I did. He then topped up the glass. What a nice man. It wasn't bad beer either. I looked at the inscription over the fireplace, some of the locals turned toward me, half smiling a greeting. "What does it say," I nodded in the direction of the fireplace, instantly

33

realisingthat every visitor from Land's End to John O'Groats must ask the same question.

"Oh, that, it roughly translates to—'Make Your Own Time Because There Will Come a Day When There Will Be No Time' I don't think anybody really knows what it means, although this lot sat here will spend all day supping and arguing about it." The locals grinned back at him, "Nowt else to do," said one. Somebody else said something in Welsh.

"Right, ta, I'll just take these outside—nice beer," I turned towards the door, wondering if they were having me on, the inscription probably said, 'We Don't Serve Alcohol To People Under The Age Of Eighteen' or something like that.

Prue looked quite comfy with her feet up, her eyes were back to normal. "The locals seem pretty friendly," I said sitting down next to her.

"Hmmm," she was miles away, "Right grab a butty, I wan't to talk to you, and don't interrupt like you usually do."

"Yes Dear."

"And stop saying that as well."

I started eating, this was nice, cheese and pickle and a half of real draught ale outdoors and an interesting conversation into the bargain, what more could a man ask for? Just one thing, I had forgot my cigars.

Prue took a sip of her Coke, "I'm glad we're away from there. I don't know if it was me but something strange happened."

"You can say that again," I replied.

"When you said you could just imagine the miners outside their cottages—I could see them—and their wives and kids. When I looked through the letterbox of the bungalow—and don't start taking the Mickey—there was a man in the hall, about 60 I'd say, he had his back to me and he was winding up the grandfather clock."

Prue was trembling slightly so I put my arm around her, she was definitely not joking.

She went on, "He turned round, he mouthed the words 'What time is it?' to me. I didn't even have to look at my watch, I just knew it was 1 o'clock.

"Hey!" I interrupted, "That was the time on the clock face when I took the flash photo."—I realised what I had said, I HAD seen the clock in the light of the flash but all my reasoning told me it was just a figment of my imagination, I felt a slight prickle in the nape of my neck as the hairs stood up ever so slightly.

"So what you're saying is—that you saw the clock that I saw being wound up by the man in the hall?" said Prue.

"Well you could say that, but I'm not too sure now." I sank half the bitter.

"Did you or didn't you?" Prue said grimly.

I thought back over the last half-hour's events. "Yes I did, but I didn't see the man."

"Good, then I'm not going bonkers—Dick, things like that don't happen every day do they?"

"No they don't love." I finished off the beer, "Are you ready to carry on?"

"Yeah, come on, let's go."

I took the glasses back into the pub, the landlord still stood behind the bar grinning from ear to ear, "Was that OK then," he enquired.

"Brill, I could have a few more but I'll be peeing all afternoon—by the way, that bungalow that's for sale down the road, is anyone living there?"

The landlord looked at me for what seemed like ages, then as if coming out of a trance, said, "Nah, feller snuffed it, only 60 an' all."

The faint prickle came back to the back of my neck.

After saying cheers to the landlord, I came outside to find Prue ready to carry on.

We started off up the road in silence. I found the blue sky and green mountains surrounding us strangely comforting. We had walked for about half a mile when I told her what the landlord had said.

"I told you he was about 60," she said almost as a matter of fact. "There's something else though."

"What."

"When you get to 60 you're gonna look just like him."

The hairs on the back of my neck stood up good style. This was one strange weekend.

We carried on until the road merged into a lane and then into a well defined footpath. The path led us into the open quarry which dominated the skyline with huge grey moody-looking rocks. We then started the ascent up into the hillside and stopped for a break nestling into the rocks, it was a perfect day. Prue cracked open a Coke. Prue leaned back and stretched her legs, looking at the grey monoliths that lay and stood around her.

"This rock must have lay for ages under the ground until the miners came and uncovered it," she said. "Do you think that it knew it had been exposed to the outside world, Dick?"

"Course not," I replied.

"I mean—do you think that it could have been ever-so-slightly aware that the sun was shining on it or that the rain was falling on it, for instance?"

"Well it would warm up or cool down I suppose," was all I could answer.

Prue placed her hand on the large boulder next to her, "Hmmm, it's on a journey isn't it?"

"What do you mean, 'on a journey,'" I sniggered.

"From the past to the future. It's been in a dark place for millions of years until some Welshman brought it out into the light."

"Well I can't argue with that," I replied, "are we going for the top then?"

We carried on until we were both proudly standing at the highest point of the quarry and took in the view of Betsy Coed spread before us—I put my arm around Prue's waist as we stood staring out in silence. I looked at my watch, it was time to make tracks back to the car, it would be dusk in about three hours.

The descent was quick and we were soon on the path, heading towards the pub, then we were on the road. After another half hour I knew that the little house with slate sills would be coming up. "We'll be approaching that house in a few minutes," I said.

"Oh, it's OK now," said Prue quiet cheerfully.

I didn't ask her what she meant, she was tying me up in riddles today. After the footbridge and round the bend the house came into view, it was in long shadow and looked quite beautiful. "You know, I could quite easily retire there," I said.

"Yes, you probably will," replied Prue.

She was at it again.

We were walking past the house now but none of us felt the urge to go up the path or even into the garden. We walked on for the next hour until we got back to the car, tired and happy. Prue would soon be fast asleep in the passenger seat as I drove home listening to the radio, I made a mental note to make sure I got a radio cassette for the car.

We journeyed home on a clear lovely evening with near empty roads. I was soon in my armchair with a whiskey and tonic by my side. I had my walking diary open ready to make an entry of the day's events.

"Shall I put the strange bits in?" I asked Prue.

"Yes," she replied emphatically, "I want you to make an accurate note . . . you never know if it will come in handy for the future."

"You're full of mysterious statements today, I said.

"Something's happened today, Dick—I don't know what it is but I think things are going to change."

I didn't answer and made the entries in the diary, the words seemed to flow and I ended up with the most accurate entry of all the trips we had been on in years of walking.

Soon it was time for bed, after putting on the alarm for work in the morning.

CHAPTER 4

After what seemed like minutes, the alarm was ringing merrily and it was time to be up for work, after my usual exercises and brekkie I was on my way, with the usual cloud of depression settling around me.

You see, it wasn't the job that got me down, it was the person I had to work with—a large woman called Canbara. Canbara was grey-haired 56-year know it all that had got through life by blundering and blustering mixed with a huge dollop of bombastic kidology. She looked and behaved like the sheepdog on the Dulux adverts. Canbara was always there before everyone else, making you always feel as though you were late, because she had already done half an hours work before 8:30. Canbara was always right and never listened to any new ideas from her staff, because she felt threatened (she wasn't a very literate person). Canbara believed that the male of the species was definitely inferior and that she could be a joiner, plumber, electrician or a fighter pilot—which was funny because she seemed to employ all of these from the Yellow Pages (except for the fighter pilot of course) or she would be helped out of a mess by one of her brothers. She wouldn't let anyone else answer the phone, so it seemed to head office and the rest of the outside world that Canbara was the only worker there—when you went to work you entered Canbara's domain—and I was stuck with her in the same room for seven and a half hours a day.

I sometimes felt sorry for her really as she had no life beyond her cats, Hanratty and Sambo, watching television and Tesco's supermarket, she was a vegetarian and avid vitamin pill popper, thinking that they would guarantee her immortality, as far as I know she had never had a relationship with another person outside of 'the Family' she had phobias of every sort coming out of her ears. She thought that nobody knew how old she was, not knowing that all the rest of the staff had known her exact birth date for years.

She let me into the bright print room that was our workplace, it wasn't a bad place actually, compared to some of the pits I had worked in during my printer's career. As usual I had to make the first remark of the day.

"Morning, Canbara, did you have a good weekend?"

This was met with the usual sigh or shrug of the shoulders, which actually meant that she had probably done exactly the same as last weekend or the one before that and so on. Her three-year-old car had an amazing 5000 miles on the clock (it wasn't even run in for God's sake). As usual she was making up an order ready for the courier with the usual air of 'If I wasn't here this place would close down for sure.' And as usual I wouldn't know what was going on until I asked. Ah well, it was a job I suppose, but how long I could put up with it I wasn't sure. I thanked God for people like Reg and Prue to keep me from going insane.

"The senior manager is coming down today with some news," said Canbara without looking up from the order sheet in front of her. Well at least she had told me in advance which was quite unusual for her.

"Oh, good news I hope?" I replied, hanging my jacket up. I looked at the clock, it was 8:25, I was too damned early again I scolded to myself.

"All I know is that there are some changes to be made." Her head popped up over the order sheet . . . . well, well, Canbara had had her hair cut and styled!

"Your hair looks better like that, it takes years off you." I remarked (well at least she didn't look like Cruella anymore). I noticed that Canbara looked slightly flushed in the cheeks.

Canbara ignored the remark and got on with making up the order.

"Stott's phoned up he's going to be late again," she said primly. I suppose to somebody that had never had a holiday or been late this was tantamount to total anarchy.

God, I'm sick of it here, I thought.

I drifted through the rest of the morning, thinking about the strange weekend I had had, first with Reg and then on our walk, it seemed as though the whole few days had been spent in a dream, I made a mental note to clear it with Prue to nip round to Reg's on the following Saturday . . . .

I suddenly realised that Canbara was shouting me, my printing machine had been running and I had been immersed in my thoughts.

"Dick, here's Dennis Moogan," she shouted from her office, she was getting a bit excited like she always did when something out of the daily routine was happening. I found it hard to whip up the slightest bit of enthusiasm, as Dennis was one of the most ineffectual Senior Managers I had ever worked under, he wouldn't have lasted five minutes at the Dandy and Beano factory where I used to work before I started at this nut house. The blokes there would have torn him to shreds and had him crying into his morning coffee. But that seemed a lifetime ago now, had I really been putting up with this for nearly nine years?

Dennis entered with his usual 'everybody's happy, aren't they' look on his face, although he did look a bit nervous this time. 'No wonder' I chuckled to myself, 'who wouldn't be when faced with the prospect of seeing Canbara.'

'Morning folks.' Yes he was definitely struggling to appear cheery. Stott, who had finally turned in and Canbara's sister, Trireme had come out of their office to acknowledge Dennis. Dennis didn't ask for coffee as he usually did, he didn't notice Canbara's new hairdo either. He ushered Canbara into her office and closed the door behind them.

"What's going on?" said Stott, standing close to me.

"Dunno, probably that row you had about Trireme." Canbara had got her elderly sister a job in the office without anybody knowing and Stott had found out that Trireme was on more money than him! We had both accused Canbara of nepotism, which she didn't like big style, she had sent us to the mental equivalent of Siberia for ages after that. "Dennis usually ignores us, so it's not much different from usual." I added, turning my printing machine off in readiness for another run.

43

Stott returned to his office to put his feet up and Trireme tried to make herself look busy as usual.

Looking through the glass partition into Canbara's office, I could see that she had gone paler than usual and Dennis was sitting at her desk with a wad of papers, which he appeared to be getting mixed up. Even from 12 feet away I could see Canbara's eyes starting to widen and her pupils dilating. 'Probably another big increase in her salary,' I mused. I got on with setting up my machine for the next job.

After about 15 minutes the door to her office briskly opened and a very brisk Dennis whizzed straight over to me and said, "Er, I've been the bringer of a bit of bad news, Canbara will fill you in with the details, gotta go to Sheffield now, see you next week." He shot out of the print room and was off within seconds, leaving me poised by my machine.

Canbara walked briskly over to me.

"You'll never guess what," she said excitedly, "their bringing in a company called Squirrels to take over the filing and their moving the printing to Huddersfield."

"What," I said uncomprehendingly, "after all the hard work we've put into this place. What is it then, redundancy?"

"They've offered to take us on at Huddersfield, but I'm not going there. I'll take the redundancy."

Inwardly I was grinning my arse off. All that grafting that Canbara had done, all the holidays she had worked, which they weren't paying her for by the way, and now they were giving her the boot. Hey Ho, what goes around comes around as they say. But the best was yet to come. Squirrels were going to employ Stott as the manager of the filing department.

My part of the redundancy was to take my machine and as much ink and paper I could and set up my own business, all for the princely sum of £1! I was losing my job, but I felt happy and was more than ready to rise to a new challenge. I couldn't wait to get home and tell Prue the good news.

Scott came into the print room grinning from ear to ear. "Yeeessss! I'm gonna be my own boss he chortled.

"Congratulations," I said, "I'm happy for you."

That evening saw me measuring up my garage ready for the installation of the printing machine.

"There's just one problem," said Prue, "You haven't any customers.

"Not yet," I replied, "but I reckon that we will be so cheap that clients will be gagging for it, we have virtually no overheads."

Well dear reader, a fortnight went slowly by, and there I was with all the equipment loaded onto a van ready to take home with me, I was out on my ear and that was to be the last I was going to see of Canbara, who was still reeling with the shock of losing her job. The bigger you are the harder you fall.

The machine and a small power guillotine and platemaker were installed in my garage with plenty of room to work in and store the paper and ink.

Now what? I had to get out there and find some people who needed letterheads and business cards, etc.

I started by going to my car insurance company. I succeeded in getting an interview with their general manager Tom Barnes. "Well what's the price of your two-color letterheads," he asked.

"I can do them for £15 a thousand," I replied.

"What," he said surprisingly, "that's well cheaper than we are paying at the moment. I'll order 15 thousand."

I came out of his office with a huge grin on my kisser and an order for letterheads, compliment slips and business cards. Time to look up my contacts in the trade. I went to a graphics studio and had the negatives I needed made up. I could make my own printing plates in my garage.

I named my printing company RP Print, the RP stood for Rick and Prue. That afternoon I started printing my first job as an independent printer. I was printing money. As I was working my thoughts turned to Reg. I had not seen him for a while as I had been so busy, so I promised myself I would give him a ring that evening. The day just flew past and I had my stationery all boxed up and ready for delivery.

I rang Reg's number. "Hello," he answered. "It's me, Rick," I replied. "I was wondering if you were all right for a meet at the weekend."

"I'll say I am. I can't wait to tell you my latest relativistic theory as to where Einstein got it wrong," he babbled excitedly.

"If you say so," I replied. "See you tomorrow at about seven then."

"OK," said Reg. "See you at seven, God I'm so excited."

As I put the phone down I couldn't help but think he was one crazy son of a bitch. I wonder what he had to say? Probably a load of crap.

CHAPTER 5

The week just flew by, I had got two more customers, one a photocopy engineer and the other a signmakers. I had earned 350 quid up to now, I was well chuffed. It soon got round to Saturday evening, and there I was standing outside Reg's front door.

I knocked. No answer. I knocked again still no answer. I went to the window and peered inside Reg's front room. The room was illuminated in a blue glowing light. I peered in closer. I couldn't believe my eyes, Reg was materializing out of thin air until he stood there as if nothing had happened!

It must be the pills I was taking for blood pressure I thought, they're making me hallucinate or something. With a slightly shaking hand I knocked again, this time Reg answered promptly.

"Come in," he said breathlessly.

'What was that blue light in your room Reg,' I said curiously.

'Oh that, it was just an effect caused by traveling at relative rest to the universe.'

'I've just seen you appear out of thin air," I said with a slight hint of hysteria in my voice.

'Yes, that's right. Why don't you crack open one of those cans you brought with you, I sure as hell could do with a drink. And I'll tell you everything. Besides, where have you been this past month, I haven't seen hide nor hair of you for ages?'

"I've been extremely busy, Reg, very busy indeed.' I pulled the ring pull on one of the cans of Boddies that I had brought with me. I observed that once again I had forked out for booze for Reg. This was typical of him, he would never think of coming round to my place to visit me.

Reg settled down into one of his shabby armchairs and took a swig of his beer. I sat down on the sofa and noticed several sheets of A4 paper on the coffee table in front of him. I picked them up. On them were scribbled masses of arithmetical formulae.

'Where did you get these Reg,' I said enquiringly.

"Oh, those, I wrote them.'

'You wrote them,' I laughed.

'Yes I did, they're quantum equations, it's a piece of piss once you get the hang of it.'

'You've been writing quantum equations,' I said disbelievingly.

'Course I have, I've been reading this book called 'Quantum Mechanics For Dummies.' It's easy!'

I couldn't believe it. Reg couldn't have actually written real mathematical formulae, could he? Only the greatest mathematicians could do that.

'But how did you get the expertise to write them?' I replied. 'Only trained scientists can do that.'

'You see, of ye of little faith, I got so gripped by reading my first book on relativity, that it inspired me so greatly that I wanted to read more and more about it, including Einstein's actual equations. I found out it was quite easy once you got the hang of it.'

'Once you got the hang of it?' I breathed.

I was a great fan of Albert's Theory of Relativity myself. But I must admit I couldn't understand the mathematics behind it, except good old $e=mc^2$. I was in complete and utter amazement. Surely Reg couldn't understand such great math.

I took a large gulp of beer, 'Listen Reg how come I saw you materialize out of thin air?'

'Wait and be patient, all will become clear in a few minutes.'

Reg began rummaging in the sideboard drawer.

'What are you doing Reg,' I queried.

'I'm looking for a pencil, I'm sure there was one in here somewhere—ah, there it is, all I need now is some blank paper.' Reg finally sat down with a few sheets of A4 and his pencil.

'What's the fastest thing in the universe?'

"Why, it's a photon which travels at the speed of light 186,000 miles a second, although there are sub-atomic particles - the neutrino and the tachyon - which in theory travel faster than the speed of light. The theory is that they travel so fast that they enter the fifth dimension for a number of nano seconds, thus giving the impression that they travel faster than C.'

'Yes, but the speed of light is accord ng to Einstein.'

'What do you mean ACCORDING to Einstein,' I said sarcastically.

'Wait have patience, now then we also know that when light enters a medium like water or glass it slows down. When it exits the medium it carries on at C as in Einstein's equation. But it doesn't accelerate to C it leaves instantly at the constant speed of C, in fact all light photons leave their source at the speed C without accelerating.'

'Yes I agree there," I said taking a swig of beer.

'But again this is according to Einstein.'

"Yes, that's right. It's fact, and proveably true."

'Now, remember the Michelson and Morely experiment where they tried to detect the so called ether that was thought at the time to be all pervading through space. They didn't detect the ether so they assumed that the speed of C was always constant with respect to the observer no matter the observers relative speed or direction of motion, agreed?'

"Right again,' I replied, Reg had certainly been doing his homework.

'So this brings me to my next point. What is the fourth dimension?'

'Time I suppose.'

'Correct, time flows from the past to the present and is embedded in our three dimensional universe. The only way we can get anywhere near the concept of time is to measure its flow by using devices like timepieces like atomic clocks and so on.

'Now, suppose we had an imaginary sealed box and took all the air out of it what would we have then?'

'A vacuum,' I replied.

'Wrong,' said Reg.

'Wrong?' I retorted.

'Yes that's right you're wrong, the latest theory is, is that electrons and positrons are created and annihilated in infinitely small periods of time inside the box.'

'Well, I didn't know that," I said rather peevishly.

'Now we come to the crux of the matter. Here's where Einstein got it wrong!'

I leaned forward expectantly.

'The speed of light, C, is not the fastest thing in the universe it is the ABSOLUTE REST of the universe, for instance when an electron moves from one orbit to another of an atoms nucleus it creates a photon, which immediately stands still and the universe flows past it. So the observer interprets this as the speed of C.'

'No sorry Reg, I'm not having that,' I replied.

'Look at it this way,' said Reg, 'Imagine a fast flowing stream. You throw a stone in it and immediately the ripples are formed they flow past the observer at the speed of the river's flow. What I'm saying is this, The river is at absolute rest so the speed of light is represented by the flow of the river and the pebble moves away from the ripples at C. I know it sounds a bit strange but I can show you the proof of it in two ways, first there's the mathematical proof and secondly there is the physical proof, hence you saw me materialize.'

I replied, 'Well, I did see you appear I suppose, but I'm not buying your theory, and are you sure you have the math, which I have no idea about, to prove it.

'Well,' answered Reg, 'The truth of the matter is this, C is now interpreted as the ether that Michelson and Morely were looking for. It can also be represented as the fifth dimension, the observer perceives the effect of the fifth dimension as C.

'You see,' he went on, 'if you believe and I mean TRULY believe in the fifth dimension. You can move within it, and time and space have no boundaries for the atoms that make up your being. God, I have seen wonderful things Dick, I have seen stars being created to the South of Orion's belt and have journeyed to the centre of the Pliades were there are a hundred suns in the sky, I have been to the centre of our galaxy and observed the great black hole that exists there.'

'Whoa Reg,' I replied, 'I cannot believe it is true what you're saying, when I leave can I take your equations with me?'

'By my guest,' he said smugly.

I intended taking them to Dr. Alan Chipman who was the chairman of the Walford Astronomical Society. If anyone could make head or tail of them, he could.

Reg was scribbling furiously on the sheets of paper.

'I've done some diagrams for you to show Dr. Chipman as well.'

Again I couldn't make any sense of them. 'I don't think there is any validation in your theory Reg, you can't be correct.' But I had a strange nagging doubt in my mind.

'Well, we'll let Dr. Chipman be the decider of that,' Reg replied. 'I have complete and utter fa th in my calculations.'

'Reg, could you do one thing for me? Let me see you dematerialise once more.'

'OK, I will. It's no problem.'

Reg stood up in the middle of the room. He closed his eyes and a frown appeared on his brow. The room started to radiate an intense blue light, and a quick as a flash Reg disappeared! Approximately ten seconds later he materialized back into the room.

'It's a great illusion Reg, but one which any magician can do.' But I still had that nagging doubt in my head.

'I've just been to the bottom of the street and back.' Said Reg with an air of supreme confidence. 'There's a bunch of kids annoying old Percy down there.'

'Right, I'm off,' I said, preparing to go. 'I'll see you at the weekend Reg.'

I left Reg's house feeling a strange sense of excitement like a kid before Christmas, when I got to the end of the street sure enough there was a bunch of yobs running poor old Percy ragged.

'Piss off you lot, what do you think you are doing harassing an old age pensioner like that,' Percy must have been 90 at least. He had been a prisoner of war, held by the Japs.

'They've broken my window,' said Percy.

'Get going the lot of you or I'll call the police,' I shouted.

'Get stuffed,' said one of the yobs, 'or we'll batter you.'

I suddenly realised that I was well outnumbered by these dickheads, and if anything started I could easily get a good hiding. I resolved to walk away from them.

'That's right, bugger off you twat,' said one of the yobs.

I bit my lip and carried on walking to shouts of abuse from the yobs. They didn't follow me and I didn't want them to know where I lived. But I was raging inside having to leave Percy at their mercy.

I was soon home. I got on the phone to the police straightaway, although I doubted whether they would do anything.

'Honestly, the kids today, they behave like a bunch of retards,' I said to Prue as she entered the room.

'I hope you didn't get involved,' said Prue, entering the room. 'You know what kids are like nowadays they can lead you a dog's life.'

'No I didn't,' I replied, 'But I could quite easily have punched their daft heads in.'

'Oh yeah,' she said, 'And then they'll have you for assault, anyway forget that for now, a bloke has been on the phone asking for a price on 40,000 A5 leaflets, single color.'

My brain immediately clicked into printer's mode. I could do them 2-up on A4 for £10 a thousand. I picked up the phone and gave the customer the estimate, he was delighted at the price and gave the order straight away, I was to pick up a sample leaflet in the morning.

'You're back early,' said Prue.

I resolved not to tell Prue about Reg. It wouldn't make any sense to her anyway.

I phoned Walford's observatory to find out when Dr. Chipman would be there. I was informed that he would be visiting the next day. I poured myself a whiskey and one for Prue (white wine) and settled down in the armchair with Reg's diagrams and equations. It might as well have been written in Chinese for all the sense it made to me. I went to bed early that night and dreamt I was flying over the city like Peter Pan.

CHAPTER 6

The next day I picked up the sample leaflet and had the negative of it done so I could make a printing plate. Apparently the bloke had been recommended to me by the signmaker. Evening soon approached.

At about 7:30 I arrived at the observatory which housed an 18-inch refracting telescope that had been donated by Jodrell Bank.

'Is Dr. Chipman available,' I asked one of the young lads seated at the computer.

'He'll be here any minute now,' he replied.

Sure enough after five minutes the great man arrived. 'Hello boys and girls,' he said with a broad grin. I suppose you could describe Dr. Chipman as 'portly,' 'It's going to be a fine night for observing.'

Dr. Chipman wore a dark blue suit with a waistcoat complete with fob watch and bow tie.

'Er, Dr. Chipman. Do you think I could have five minutes of your time, it's just that I have this friend who has an alternative theory of the General Theory of Relativity.

'Ah hah,' he laughed, 'this should be very interesting. Tell me more my boy, tell me more.'

I explained Reg's theory as best I could particularly the bit about the speed of light being the relative rest of the universe.

Dr. Chipman frowned and then said 'In my opinion old boy, I have never heard anything so full of poppycock in my life, it is complete and utter rubbish.'

'Here's the maths to go with it and some diagrams, too,' I said, I could feel my cheeks reddening.

"Done by the same person I suppose," he said, "Let's see now, what do we have here."

His eyes began to widen, he put on his specs. His hand began to shake ever so slightly. 'Why this math is the most elegant I have seen in a long time, it seems to bear out the fact that your friend's theory is correct! I shall have to discuss this with Professor Pringle to see what he makes of it, leave me your telephone number and I will contact you in due course.'

As quick as a flash I whipped out one of my business cards, and gave it to him.

I felt elated, could Reg be right after all? I had omitted to tell Dr Chipman about Reg dematerializing, perhaps he would conclude that for himself. I couldn't wait for the weekend to arrive so I could tell Reg the good news—all I had to wait for now was for Professor Pringle to corroborate the theory too.

I spent the next day running off the A5 leaflets, they were for a wheely bin cleaners who lived in a caravan site on the outskirts of the city, yes folks I was as totally happy as I had been for years. This beat working with Canbara any day of the week.

Prue came into the garage with the cordless phone. 'It's for you, a Dr. Alan Chipman.'

'Well, my boy, I am glad to inform you that your friend's theory is born out by his calculations. He would be best served if he wrote it up and submitted it for publication in the journal 'Nature'. I would be interested to meet your friend at his earliest convenience.'

'I think that I could arrange a meeting for Friday,' I replied. I could feel my arse tightening with anticipation. This will blow Reg's mind I thought.

'Alright, do your best my boy, contact me as soon as you can, here's my phone number.' He rang off.

I immediately got on the phone to Reg. 'Reg,' I gasped, 'You'll never guess what, Dr. Chipman is gagging for your theory, he wants to meet you and wants you to put pen to paper and publish it in the journal 'Nature.'"

'Told you so, didn't I,' came the smug reply, 'But just one thing.'

'What's that Reg?'

'Don't tell him about the dematerializing bit, that's to be our secret.'

'OK Reg, whatever you say, see you Friday evening,' I rang off.

That nagging doubt in my mind had all but disappeared to be replaced by such a feeling of elation and pride in Reg's achievement. Old lazybones Reg, writing a paper for 'Nature,' who would credit that? Meanwhile Reg was as smug as ever and completely unfazed by the whole affair.

CHAPTER 7

The next day I delivered the leaflets after some difficulty finding the correct caravan to deliver them to. The bloke paid up there and then, 400 smackaroos, piece of cake! Friday was a long day, it seemed to crawl past, we had arranged for me to pick up Dr. Chipman and Professor Pringle and take them both to Reg's house. Here it was at last, a meeting of three great minds.

We all got seated on Reg's knackered three-piece suite. They started the debate. Almost immediately I was out of my depth, the main part of the debate appeared to revolve around Reg's postulation of a five dimensional universe and it's consequences for string theory, gravity, quantum mechanics and matter itself. At no point was the fact that Reg had dematerialized the atoms that made up his body, mentioned. Reg was scribbling on his sheets of paper again, he triumphantly held it up for us to see.

'Why, that's the mathematical proof that the fifth dimension that we perceive as the speed of light exists,' said an overjoyed Professor Pringle.

'By Jove, it certainly does,' said Dr. Chipman enthusiastically. 'It's similar to the old stationary ether theory, but I wonder if atoms can exist within this dimension.'

Reg shot me a look as if to say 'they're getting close to the dematerializing part of my theory.'

I nodded back to confirm that I understood. 'No they can't, because they would be annihilated by particles of antimatter that exist there,' Reg said as he scribbled some more.

He held up the sheet of paper to show the new equations.

'Ah, yes I see,' said Dr. Chipman. 'Yes, that's clear enough,' said Professor Pringle.

"Well, I think that's as much as we can discuss for tonight, as for me I'm going to call a meeting of the Walford Astronomical Society next week and tell them this most exciting news,' said Dr. Chipman, rubbing his hands with glee.

Reg and I showed the two gentlemen out.

'Why don't you want them to know the main part of your theory Reg,' I asked.

'Because we don't want all and sundry transporting themselves all over the universe now do we?' he replied. 'I gave them a load of mathematical garbage, and they fell for it. Now then do you *truly, truly believe in my theory*?'

'Yes, I can honestly say that I do Reg,' I replied.

'Very well,' he said seriously, 'let's go on a little trip then. Now, you must think hard about the theory and the speed of light being the relative rest of the universe, but remember if you find yourself among people you must not touch them or you might kill them, it will be like the ripple effect in the stone and the fast flowing stream analogy. You will cause a ripple in the fabric of space time. Now think hard. And another thing, think of where you would like to materialize to.'

I concentrated with all my might on Reg's theory and thought of his front room or parlor as he liked to call it. Two minutes went by, nothing happened, I thought harder, to my amazement the room started glowing blue and I could feel a tingling sensation throughout my body. I held my hand up in front of my face, it was becoming opaque! My hand disappeared altogether. I then realised I was in Reg's front room. I noticed that his baby grand wall clock had stopped. Christ, I could transcend space and time! I then thought of Reg's back room and in a second I was back, with a broad grin on my face, I felt as if all my Christmases had come at once.

'That was fantastic Reg,' I said gleefully. I walked out of his back room and into the front, the wall clock was ticking away merrily.

I went back into the back room. 'That was just mind blowing, Reg.'

'I know, it's great isn't it.' Reg was grinning broadly as well as I. 'Can't you think of something more exciting than my front room?'

So it was no magician's trick at all. I had really transported myself through the fabric of space time and into the fifth dimension.

'I think I've had enough excitement for today, Reg,' I said. 'I think I am going home now.'

'OK then, but remember, this is our little secret, right.'

'Sure thing Reg,' I replied. I stepped out of Reg's house into the cool night, it was clear and the stars were shining brightly. I looked up at them, yes the world, no, the universe was my oyster. As I was about to get into my Metro I heard the sound of breaking glass. It was Percy's window again, so the little bastards were back. I jumped into my car and drove straight at them, they scattered in all directions before running off. I got out of the car and knocked on Percy's door, he answered it in floods of tears. 'Why won't they leave me alone?' he sobbed.

'Never mind Percy,' I sympathized. 'Get yourself in and phone your insurance hotline, I'm sure they will send someone to replace your window.' I could feel the rage rising up again inside me.

I was soon home, I could hardly drive with the excitement of the evening. I resolved to teleport myself the next day. In the meantime it was time for a whiskey, or two.

'You've had two more enquiries for some stationery, Dick,' said Prue, taking a sip of her whiskey and tonic. I decided to tell Prue all about Reg's theory, leaving out the dematerializing bit. 'It's all Greek to me,' she said. 'Anyway I'm off to bed, you look as though you could do with an early night yourself,' she said, with a naughty glint in her eye.

I poured myself another whiskey and sat down in my favourite armchair, thoughts about Reg and Percy racing through my head. I thought about what Reg had said, 'If you find yourself among people you must not touch them or you might kill them.' Hhmm, that was worth noting. I went to bed, Prue was fast asleep, so I cuddled up her lovely bum. I fell into a doze, still thinking of the theory of relativity, I wonder what Einstein would have made of it all?

CHAPTER 8

After a night of fitful sleep I awoke to find Prue up and ready for the day. 'Would you like a fry-up for breakfast?' she queried.

'I certainly would,' I replied.

After a breakfast of sausage, bacon and beans, I was feeling good. First job was to phone back the two customers that had made enquiries about business cards. One of them was the world famous clothes supplier Henri Boyd! I made arrangements to see one at two and the other at four that day. I also had to pick up the photographs that we had taken on our last walking trip, so I went to the photo lab to collect them. I was sat in the car as I thumbed through them, when I got to the photo of the bungalow's hallway it showed the clear outline of a figure of a man winding up the grandfather clock! 'Well I'll be damned,' I thought. 'Wait till I show Prue these, she's gonna love this one.'

I got home for about 12, and was showing the photographs to Prue, 'Look at this one,' I babbled excitedly, showing her the photograph of the man in the hallway.

'Yes I know, I saw him as well,' she replied calmly. She seemed completely unfazed about the photograph. 'Let's go back there this weekend.'

'OK,' I replied. 'We'll go on Sunday.'

That afternoon I was at Henri Boyds. I was shown into a plush office to see their buyer, as soon as I mentioned the price (£20 for 500) he looked at me fixedly and said, 'I hope you can do them with the same quality that we are accustomed to.'

'If you're not happy, I won't charge you a penny,' I replied. They were to be done in gold and reflex blue, both of which I already had as part of my redundancy package.

'Very well, I'll order 10 lots for our reps and managers, there will be some letterheads as well if you do a satisfactory job.'

I left his office with a grin on my kisser, this printing game was a piece of cake, time to call on my next customer who turned out to be a taxi driver. He wanted 1000 single color, I said I could do them for £50, hey, ho, it's swings and roundabouts I suppose.

The next day I went to the art studio for my negatives, the negs for Henri Boyd were 10-up and the ones for the taxi driver were 4-up. It cost me £15 for the three of them. So I calculated I should make £235 on the deal. Piece of cake. I ran them off the same day. I was guillotining them the next day when Prue came into the garage with the cordless phone, 'it's Reg for you.'

'Hi Reg, how's things,' I said.

'Can you come down to mine,' he replied. 'Something's going on here.'

'Like what?' I replied.

'I've got newspaper reporters on my front doorstep, and I don't know what to do.'

'Oh, my God, have you started on the paper for 'Nature' yet, Reg?'

'Yes I have, as it happens, but what do I do about these reporters?'

'You'll have to grant them an interview I suppose, look, wait till I get there and we'll invite them in.'

'I can't be doing with all this palaver, Dick, it's getting right on my wick.'

Reg was always the loner and very private, so he couldn't deal with any fuss. He would feel better if I came round for moral support. 'I've got to go round and see Reg,' I shouted to Prue.

'What, again. You might as well move in with him.'

'He's got the media on his doorstep and, you know what Reg is like, he can't cope.'

'OK, then, but don't be late for tea,' Prue warned.

I jumped in the Metro and shot around to Reg's, it only took 10 minutes. Sure enough there was a gaggle of newsmen outside Reg's front door, a few of his neighbours were standing by as well.

'Hello, gentlemen,' I said as I got out of the car, 'I suppose you want to meet my friend Reg do you?'

'Yes please,' said one, 'I'm from the Daily Mail, 'And I'm from the Daily Telegraph,' said another. 'I'm the science correspondent from the Guardian,' said yet another.

'You do know that Reg is going to publish in 'Nature,' don't you?'

'Yes we do,' said the Guardian reporter. 'But if Mr, ah, what's his name? could give us a brief outline of the new theory, we'd be most grateful.'

'Actually, it's Mr. Reginald Stein you'll be speaking to, and where did you learn about Mr. Stein's work exactly?'

'From the Walford Astronomical Society, they called an extraordinary meeting yesterday to discuss the theory. And one of the reporters from the Walford City Reporter was there,' piped up the man from the Telegraph. 'He then informed us.'

'Right, you lot wait here and I'll see if Reg will see you.' I lifted up Reg's letterbox flap and shouted, '"Reg, it's me, Dick, let me in.'

The door opened a crack and Reg peered round it. 'Quick, come in,' he said breathlessly.

I squeezed in through the doorway, I could see that Reg was quite agitated.

'I don't like this one bit,' he said.

'You'll have to grant them an interview,' I replied. 'Now pour yourself a stiff whiskey and try to calm down and when you're ready we'll let them in.'

As usual Reg poured one for himself and completely ignored me. He downed his drink in one. 'I think I'll have another,' he said.

'No you don't, you don't want to be out of control when you let the newsmen in, do you? Now go and let them in.

We showed the assembled reporters into Reg's front room, a couple of flashbulbs went off as we ushered them in. Reg held his hand up to his face. I could see he was going through an ordeal. The interview went pretty well as Reg got over his nerves and he was soon in his stride as he explained Einstein's theory of Relativity and the changes he had made to it, all the while trying to keep it as simple as he could. It was soon question time for the journalists.

The reporter from the Mail held up his hand, 'This theory is all very well, but have you got any mathematical proof to go with it?'

'Yes, I have' said Reg as he held up a sheet of A4 which was crammed with Math symbols. 'And I've got another nine sheets to prove my theory, and several diagrams, too.' He held up the sheet for the newsmen to read.

'Why, this is brand new mathematics,' said the science correspondent from the Guardian.

'Yes I know,' replied Reg. 'It has to be, just as Quantum Mechanics has to have it's own brand of math as proof of the theory so does my theory of relativity.

'It's all a load of bollocks to me,' said the reporter from the Star.

At last the newsmen were satisfied as they filed out to make up their reports.

'Thank God that's over,' said Reg.

'I have to go home now, Reg,' I said. 'I'll just call on Percy to see if he's alright.' I got in the car, and pulled up outside Percy's. I knocked on his door, after a couple of minutes he opened it slowly. 'I'm just calling to see if you're OK, Percy' I said loudly, as I knew Percy was just a tad deaf.

'Yes, I'm OK,' he said, 'I've had the windows repaired as you can see, it's quiet now, but that's because the buggers are still at school.'

'Well, as long as you're alright Percy.'

I headed for home. When I got there Prue was cooking tea. 'I'm doing your favourite, pork chops and chips.'

"Ooh great.' I enthused, 'I'll just grab a shower. While I was showering my thoughts turned towards Reg (as if they hadn't been anywhere else) what next for Reg. I supposed it will be the lecture circuit and television no doubt. I toweled off and went downstairs for tea.

CHAPTER 9

The next day I delivered the business cards to Henri Boyds, 'Just leave them there on the table,' said the buyer and send us your invoice. 'We'll discuss the letterheads at a later date.' So, they weren't going to pay on delivery, typical of big business. I carried on to meet the taxi driver by the side of the park. 'These are great,' he said. 'I'll be needing some more in a few weeks.'

He handed over the money promptly, Ah well, at least I was up £50 on the day.

As I journeyed home I decided to call Reg, as soon as I got in I picked up the phone and dialed his number, Prue was out shopping. 'Hello Reg, it's me Dick, how's it going?'

'I have nearly finished the paper for 'Nature' and Scientific American want me to do an article for them, oh, and the BBC want me for an interview on their breakfast show,' said Reg excitedly, 'Will you come with me Dick?'

'You're quite the celebrity aren't you Reg,' I replied. 'And yes, of course I will come with you. Do you need anything.'

'Yes some cans of Boddingtons.'

I rang off. The crafty bastard, he'd got me to buy his ale again, but I wasn't fussed, I was happy for Reg he deserved it. So I nipped round to the off license and bought two four-packs of Boddies, one for Reg and one for me. When I got home the house was empty, so I decided to go into the garage and clean my printing press, as I wiped the ink off my thoughts turned towards dematerializing again. I stood still and thought of the theory and my belief in it then I thought of the bottom of the road where I lived. Sure enough the air around me began to radiate with blue light and I started to fade. I materialized at the bottom of my road, one of my neighbours was in his front garden mowing his lawn, he was frozen in the action of mowing. 'Of course,' I thought, 'time is standing still so everything I observe is doing the same.' But I could move around at will within the five-dimensional time frame. I walked slowly up to my neighbour who was like a statue, a drop of perspiration on his brow. I walked in a circle around him, a cat was motionless, caught in the act of running across the road. I willed myself back into my garage, I really will have to transpose myself to somewhere more exciting next time I thought. But what if I couldn't get back, I must admit I was a big apprehensive about it.

I locked up the garage and went indoors to be met by Prue who had finished her shopping, 'I thought we could go out for tea tonight,' she said unpacking her bags.

'Yeah, OK, we'll go to the Barton Arms. I'm just going to grab a shower and put on a clean shirt.' Half an hour later we were on our way to the pub. When we entered we got a nice table by the window, I ordered a medium done steak for me and hake for Prue. Our conversation turned towards Reg, 'You know, Reg is getting quite famous now, even the BBC want to interview him,' I said.

'Is that so,' said Prue, 'What's all the fuss about, anyway?'

'You don't understand do you love,' I replied. 'It's one of the most fundamental theories to hit the scientific world since Einstein.'

'Yes but what difference will it make to the ordinary man in the street?'

'If you only knew.' I thought. 'Come on, let's go home.' As we journeyed home I thought about the next day, Reg should be charging a fee for his public appearances I promised myself that I would discuss it with him tomorrow. Right now I was knackered and ready for a good kip.

CHAPTER 10

The next day dawned bright and sunny, I got up, washed and got dressed, I wondered if I should wear a tie, no probably not. I went out into the crisp morning air and walked to the newsagents at the bottom of the road. When I got there I picked up a copy of the Guardian, the headline read, LAYMAN RE-WRITES EINSTEIN'S THEORY. There was a picture of Reg on the third page and quite a fair sized article, too. The Mail and the Telegraph had similar stories to tell. The Walford Advertiser's headline read, LOCAL MAN IN THEORY DISPUTE. The Daily Star read, BONKERS THEORY EXPOSED. That was typical of them I thought. I decided to purchase a copy of The Guardian. Reg's fame was spreading I thought, yes, somebody will have to start forking out for his public appearances.

I had breakfast and went round to Reg's, everything appeared OK at Percy's as I passed. The time was 7 a.m. I knocked on Reg's door as a Granada TV van pulled up outside his house. 'Can I help you?' I queried. The window wound down and a rather attractive woman poked her head out.

'Yes, I'm looking for a Mr. Reginald Stein, my name is Marcia Brookes and I'm from Granada TV. I have a show called 'Good Morning Britain' and I was wondering if Mr. Stein would like to appear on it.'

'Yes, he probably would, but how much are you willing to pay for such an appearance?' I replied.

'Are you his manager?' Marcia said.

'Well, I suppose I am.'

She got out of the van, showing a shapely pair of high-heeled legs in the process, 'Well, I suppose we could run to a couple of thousand pounds for an interview on prime-time television,' she said.

'Call it two thousand five hundred and you've got yourself a deal.'

'Fair enough,' she replied 'I suppose that will be acceptable.'

I realised that Reg hadn't opened his front door, so lifted the flap of his letterbox and shouted 'Reg, it's only me, Dick, hurry up or we'll be late for the interview at the BBC.'

The door opened up slowly and Reg appeared in his jim jams. 'What time is it, and who's THAT?' He cast an appreciative eye over Marcia.

'This is Marcia Brookes from GTV, she wants to interview you, I said you would be happy to for two and a half grand. She said that was OK.'

'Two and a half smackaroonies!' gasped Reg, 'I've never had that amount of money in all my life.'

'Reg you're getting to be quite famous now so people will happily pay for your appearances.'

We went inside and I put the cans of Boddies in his fridge. 'When do you want me for interview then,' Reg said eying up Marcia.

'As soon as possible, like tomorrow morning actually.'

'For you darling, anything,' Reg smarmed.

'Right Reg, when we get to the BBC I don't want you to talk to anyone until I've spoken to the producer, understand? Now get dressed and hurry up!'

Reg was still eying up Marcia, 'I don't suppose you'd like to come round for tea tonight would you?' he enquired.

'Why, of course I would,' replied Marcia 'About eight suit you?'

'Fine,' replied Reg.

Reg went upstairs to wash and change.

'Well, I'll be off then,' said Marcia, 'I'll see you sometime.'

After about 15 minutes Reg came down dressed in his best T shirt and jeans 'Where's Marcia.'

'She's had to go, I suppose she's a very busy woman,' I replied.

'She's a cracker,' said Reg, 'remind me to get some fish fingers in for tea.'

'You're not going to give her fish fingers are you Reg?'

'And chips,' retorted Reg.

We set off for the BBC studios in Manchester.

The traffic was horrendous and we arrived in the nick of time, we waited at reception after giving our names, soon a tall bloke came down the stairs and introduced himself, 'Hello, my name's Bill Baily and I'm the producer of the morning news program. We'll just get you in makeup for a quick dust down and then we're on.

'Whoa, just a minute,' I said, 'we haven't discussed fees yet.'

'Fees?'

'Yes fees. You don't expect Reg to appear for nothing do you? So how much?

'Well I suppose we could offer a thousand.'

'One thousand five hundred and you've got yourself a deal.' I was quite liking this managerial lark.

'Agreed,' said Bill.

With that we went into what appeared to be a cross between a hairdressers and a beauty parlor where a glamorous assistant gave Reg the once over with a powder brush. 'What's your name then darlin' he asked.

'June,' she replied.

'Would you care to come out with me for a drink after we've finished here?'

'No, I couldn't, I've got a boyfriend,' she giggled.

Thank God for that I thought, Reg was going woman crazy. It must be the fame thing. Bill Baily called Reg into the studio, the interview went well with Reg trying to keep it simple, he was told by the producer to leave out all the maths as his audience were mainly housewives and unemployed men. Soon it was over and Reg and I were invited to the lounge for drinks. Reg was delighted to find that they had his beloved Boddies in cans, so we both had one.

'So Dick are you Reg's manager then?' Bill enquired.

'Yes I suppose I am,' I said for the second time. 'But I own my own printing business, here's my card.' I whipped out one of my business cards pretty quick. 'Business cards are £30 for 500 for single color and £45 for two color.'

'Right I'll remember that when I need some, but we get them from the general manager who has them printed outside,' Bill said, 'I'll get you an interview with him if you like.'

'Yes that would be great,' I said. What a stroke of luck I thought, they must want thousands of business cards here not to mention letterheads.

'Well goodbye then,' said Bill. 'You're cheque will be in the post.

'Adios,' I said and ushered Reg out of the building after leaving his address at reception.

We got to the car and sat in it 'One and a half grand,' piped Reg, 'It's money for old rope.'

'You'd better open a bank account Reg, I think you're gonna need it. I'll drop you off at the precinct.'

With that I dropped Reg outside the TSB and headed for home. When I got in Prue was just putting the phone down, 'You've had another inquiry from the signmakers, it's from a sun bed parlor they want 2000 leaflets and two lots of business cards some for him and some for her, oh, and it's three color.' I got on the phone straightaway and made an appointment to see the owner that afternoon.

'I have been watching Reg on the telly,' said Prue, 'He looked proper scruffy.'

'Well scruffy or not, he's earned himself a cool £1500.' I told Prue about how I had negotiated Reg's fees.

'You'd better charge him commission,' replied Prue.

'I know, I was thinking about that myself, I'll see him tonight and discuss it with him.'

Later on in the afternoon I went to see the sun bed man about his stationery, he ordered 2000 A5 leaflets and two lots of business cards at a 1000 a time. The job would come to £230. A nice little earner.

After tea I had a quick nap and then went round to Reg's. As I entered his road I noticed that five youths were loitering outside Percy's house. 'They just won't leave the poor old bastard alone,' I thought. I pulled up outside Reg's. The GTV van was outside, of course, Marcia was down for tea. 'I won't keep you long Reg, I just want to discuss something with you, it's about your fees—seeing as I negotiated them I feel I should retain a percentage for myself,' I said as Reg opened the door.

'Marcia's here,' said Reg as he ushered me in.

Marcia was sat down on one of Reg's old armchairs, she looked gorgeous in a little black number.

'Er, we're just about to have tea,' said Reg glaring at me.

I felt as wanted as a bull in a china shop.

'Hello Marcia,' I said, 'I was just saying to Reg that I should have a cut of his fees seeing as I negotiated them, what do you think?'

'Well, I agree,' said Marcia, 'seeing as you screwed an extra 500 quid out of Granada this morning, I would suggest 20 percent would be fair.

Good on you Marcia.

'Yes, yes, anything. Now if you don't mind my fish fingers will be burning,' said an impatient Reg as he shoved me towards his front door.

'See you, Marcia,' I shouted as Reg bundled me out. 'Don't do anything I wouldn't do.' I winked at Reg, 'I'll see you at about seven tomorrow morning.'

I left Reg to lust after Marcia, 'He's getting to be quite the boy isn't he,' I thought.

I drove to the top of the street, the youths were still outside Percy's one of them was shouting something through Percy's letterbox. I drove past them—A seed of an idea grew in my mind. I parked up on some deserted waste ground just around the corner. I thought of Reg's theory and then Percy's street. Sure enough the interior of the car glowed blue and the atoms of my body disappeared. I materialized outside Percy's. The five youths were frozen in various stances, 'Well, what do we have here?' I thought as I strolled up to one of them, he was caught in the action of throwing a half brick at Percy's window. I felt a rage build up in me. "Fuckin' regard,' I thought. I thought of what Reg had said to me when I was about to take my first trip, *'Don't touch anybody as you might kill them.'*

'Well here's one for you Percy!' I drew back my fist and smacked the retard in the side of the head, to my horror his head disintegrated into a thousand blood red crystals. 'Jesus,' I thought, 'I wasn't expecting that!'

I gaped at the now headless youth, quickly in a panic I willed myself back into the car. I was shaking so much I couldn't drive, about 15 minutes passed by as I began to calm down, there was, all of a sudden, the sound of an ambulance siren coming closer, an ambulance came tearing down the main road and turned into the street followed by a police car. I waited for another 15 minutes before curiosity got the better of me and I got out of the car and casually strolled into Percy's street, people were standing by as the police were looking at the youth's decapitated body lying on the ground a large pool of blood and bits of brain was spattered on the cobbles.

And so it was, Wesley smith, or 'our Wes' as his delinquent mother Mandy liked to call him (she was nicknamed 'Randy Mandy' because she had seven kids by five different fathers) died a horrible death.

I walked up to one of the bystanders 'What happened,' I queried.

'Looks like roadkill to me,' he said.

Just then a black Ford pulled up at the scene and two big plainclothes detectives got out, Detective Inspector David Harrison and DI Donald Greaves. 'Christ would you look at that,' exclaimed DI Harrison. 'Looks like he's been hit by a truck. And what's that in his hand?'

"It's a half brick, boss,' said DI Greaves.

Turning to the assembled crowd DI Harrison said, 'OK, who saw what happened?'

The four remaining youths stepped forward, 'Us,' they said together.

Pointing to one of them DL Harrison said, 'OK, talk.'

'Yo, man we the homeboys roun' here and we wus just hangin when . . . .'

'What are you talking like a black man for?' interrupted DI Harrison, 'You're just an ordinary British white kid, so talk like one.'

The young thug hung his head and muttered, 'Well, we were standing around when all of a sudden Wes's head exploded.'

'So, there was no traffic or lorries involved then?' said DI Harrison.

'No mister, none at all.'

'Why has he got a half brick in hand?' asked DI Harrison.

'Dunno,' mumbled the youth.

'Right I want these kids down at the station for questioning.' To the assembled crowd he said, 'anybody else see anything?'

This was met by a shake of heads from the assembled people. Just then Percy came to his front door. 'What's going on?' he said.

'Looks like one of your friends has been run over,' I replied.

'Oh, goody,' said Percy.

To the other policemen DI Harrison said, 'OK lads, get forensics down here and tape off the scene.'

I walked back to the car, numb with the enormity of what I had done. I was home in ten minutes.

'Well, how did you get on then?' said Prue.

'Oh I got 20 percent,' I said woodenly, 'Reg is entertaining Marcia from GTV.'

'Huh, that's nice,' she said smiling, 'Henri Boyds have been in contact they want five thousand letterheads ASAP.'

'Right OK, I'll see them tomorrow after Reg and I have been to GTV.'

'Are you alright Dick, you look as white as a sheet?'

'Yeah I'm OK, it's just that some kid has been run over in Reg's street. He's umm, dead.'

'Oh, how awful, never mind I'll get you a nice whiskey and tonic, go and sit down.'

I sat down in my favourite armchair, my cat DJ sprang onto my lap, I downed my whiskey in one go, and instantly I felt better. The police couldn't trace the 'accident' to me could they? Prue took my glass and poured me another. My hands started to lose the slight tremble they had when I came in. I thought more logically about what had happened 'The retard had it coming.' I stroked my cat's head absentmindedly.

'I must remember to get some sausage rolls in for our trip to Wales on Sunday,' said Prue.

I went to bed that night with my head in a whirl of thoughts about the day's events. I slept fitfully.

CHAPTER 11

Soon the alarm went off, it was seven a.m. on a Friday. I got up, showered, and had some toast. I went as usual to the newsagents to get the Walford Advertiser. There was nothing in it about last nights happenings, probably too late to go to press, I thought. I skimmed through the paper and soon it was time to pick up Reg. As I turned into Reg's street the fire brigade were hosing down the cobble stones where the youth had met his death. I felt my backside contract. As usual Reg was in bed so I knocked hard and rapped his letterbox. A dozy Reg appeared in his pajamas and let me in.

'You'll never guess what,' said Reg excitedly one of those retards that were pestering Percy got his head kicked in last night, flippin' great, hey!'

'Yeah, I suppose so, perhaps now they will leave him alone. How did you get on with Marcia last night?'

'Great, she enjoyed her fish fingers and chips, so that just shows you what you know doesn't it? And, what's more she gave me a kiss goodnight.'

'You Cassenova, you,' I laughed. 'You'll be seeing her again in about an hour's time.'

'Can't wait,' he replied pouring some milk on his cornflakes.

We battled through the traffic and were soon at GTV's reception. Marcia came down to greet us, she planted a kiss on Reg's lips and gave him a big hug, there was nothing for me except for a brisk handshake. It was more of the same really, Reg went into makeup and then into the studio to be interviewed by Marcia, carefully leaving out the maths. After the show Reg and Marcia came out of the studio arm in arm.

Marcia gave Reg a big kiss and said, 'See you tonight gorgeous.'

'Gorgeous?' I thought.

'OK, Babe,' said Reg, 'See you at eight. I can't wait.'

They parted, Reg said to me, 'Marcia's coming round for a take away and a video tonight.'

'You're getting to be quite an item,' I replied.

I dropped Reg off at his house, there was now no sign of what had gone on the night before. I carried on to Henri Boydes and met their buyer. 'those business cards were great,' he said. 'I'll order 5,000 letterheads and 5,000 comp slips, here's some samples of both. I dropped the samples off at the art studio and then got the evening paper from the newsagents. The headline read: HEADLESS BODY FOUND IN WALFORD STREET. The articles read:

Police are baffled as to what happened to a youth whose body was found in Humber Street last night. The body was headless. DI David Harrison said that the injuries were so horrific that the blood stained clothing found on the culprit or in their houses or of any new dents or damage to family vehicles. It appears that the youths injuries were most likely caused by a hit and run car or van.

I could feel myself getting hot under the collar as I read the article, at least the police were looking in the wrong direction. I got in the car and headed for home, when I got in Prue was preparing tea.

'Let's have a look at the paper then,' she said. 'God that's awful, the poor boy.'

'If you only knew,' I thought.

Meanwhile at the police station DI Harrison was talking to a forensics technician, 'Well, what have you got for me?' he said.

The technician replied, 'Firstly we can rule out a hit and run accident, because there were no skid marks in the blood on the ground or on the cobbled street. Secondly we can dismiss a blow to the head with a blunt instrument, the trauma was too extensive for that. The only place where I've ever seen anything like the kind of damage we have here is when I was in the army and troops were hit in the head by a high velocity projectile like a bullet from a sniper's rifle. Or small caliber field gun round. And I can say that the youth was standing upright when his head blew up.

'When his head blew up?' retorted DI Harrison. 'You can't say that, how can a head blow up?'

'Well, all the evidence points to it,' said the technician.

'God knows what I'm going to tell the Press this afternoon,' said DI Harrison.

Prue gave me back the newspaper, on page three was an article about a family from hell who was terrorizing their neighbours and leading them a dog's life. The so called 'family' comprised of an unmarried mother and her two sons aged fifteen and fourteen. They had been damaging property and were a real pain in the arse in the neighbourhood.

'Hmm, I shall have to pay them a visit,' I thought, wait, what was I thinking? I couldn't possibly do THAT again could I?

'Come on for your tea, Dick,' shouted Prue from the kitchen.

Oooh egg and chips, delicious, all thoughts of any more vigilantism left my mind as I tucked in.

CHAPTER 12

Sunday morning broke with gorgeous sunshine and found me and Prue packing our hiking boots and rucksack into the car. We had a lunch of sausage rolls packed as well.

We made Betsy Coed within two hours and parked up at the old mill by the stream and donned our walking boots and set off for Penmachno. It was a flat walk, just as Prue liked it, so we set off down the lane. After about half an hour we passed the miner's cottages which had now been gutted and were in the process of being renovated, 'That's good,' I said, 'They'll look great when they're done.'

'Yes they will,' said Prue, 'but I still prefer the old bungalow up ahead.' We walked on up the lane, it certainly was beautiful basking in the sunshine, we were soon at the old bungalow come cottage. It was still up for sale only this time it had a notice saying 'Any reasonable offer considered.'

'I can just picture us living here Dick,' said Prue.

'Yeah, so can I,' I replied.

We both let ourselves into the front garden and peered through the front bay window. There was still the distempered walls and old linoleum on the floor.

'He's still here,' said Prue.

'Who is?' I replied.

'Why, the man who used to own it of course, but he's dead now.'

I looked at Prue, 'What could she possibly mean by that?'

We set off again down the lane until we came to the pub. 'What do you want to drink Chuck,' I said.

'Oh, just half a bitter,' said Prue.

I went in and ordered two halves of bitter, 'Hello young man. Back again are we?' said the landlord as he pulled the beer.

'Blimey, he remembered me,' I thought. 'I suppose he doesn't get many strangers in here.' The same locals were sat in the corner of the room.

'Yes, I'm hiking with my wife,' I replied. I nodded in the direction of the locals, 'How do,' they chorused. Nice friendly bunch I thought.

I took the beers out to Prue, who was unpacking the sausage rolls.

'The locals are friendly,' I said, 'And the landlord remembered me from last time we were here.

'Dick, I've been thinking about the old bungalow.'

'What about it,' I replied.

'Let's buy it!'

'Buy it, with what?' I said.

'Listen, you've got savings in the bank and I've got savings too, and they're both earning sod all interest. It would mean a small mortgage I suppose, but I reckon we could do it. After all our house is paid off now.'

'But what about the printing business?' I replied, 'It's a two hour drive to Walford from here.'

'I don't mean live here permanently, it would make a lovely holiday home.'

'The crafty little tinker,' I thought, 'she's been saving up a nest egg all these years.'

I must admit that both our savings could come to quite a sum to put down on the cottage.

'OK, I don't suppose it would do any harm to phone the estate agent and see how much they want for it,' I replied.

Prue reached out and squeezed my arm. 'You won't regret it.'

We completed our walk and stopped for a break at the foothills. 'Just think, you could ramble up the hills on your own if we bought the bungalow,' said Prue.

I was quietly warming to the idea of owning a bungalow holiday home. We completed our walk and drove home, we were both quiet, immersed in our own thoughts. When we got home we decided to discuss our finances.

"OK, how much have you got in the bank, sweetie,' I said to Prue.

"About forty thousand,' she replied.

"And I've got about seventy thousand,' I said, 'But we must keep some on one side to do up the bungalow and furnish it.'

'I've got another ten thousand in the TSB,' said Prue. 'We could use that for sundry items like a bed and carpets, etc.'

'Those floorboards will sandpaper up a treat though,' I replied. 'Anyway, let's not jump the gun, let's see what the estate agent has to say on Monday morning.'

We were both up for eight on the Monday morning and I could see that Prue was itching to phone up the estate agent in Wales.

I went down our road to the newsagents. I looked through the daily papers and decided to buy the Guardian. I walked back home, the time was nine o'clock. When I got in Prue was on the phone to the estate agents, 'OK, I see,' she said, 'alright, I'll discuss it with my husband.' She put the phone down.

'Well,' I said, 'What's the damage?'

"They want one hundred and forty thousand for it, but I reckon we could put in an offer for one hundred and thirty, after all, it's been up for sale for quite some time now.'

"Ok, do it,' I replied.

Prue got on the phone again and submitted the offer. 'They're going to ring us back after they've spoken to the vendor.'

I took my paper into the front room, on page ten there was an article with the heading: POLICE BAFFLED BY HEADLESS CORPSE, the article read.

Police have today admitted that they are completely baffled as to the cause of Wesley Smith's death in a Walford side street after his headless body was found last week. They are conducting house to house questioning in the area. Anybody with any information should ring Walford police station.

It was with great relief that that the police were found to be clueless as to what had happened. I went in the kitchen and brewed a cup of tea, 'I might pay that problem family a visit after all,' I thought.

The phone rang, 'Hello?' said Prue, 'Oh that was quick, that's great, we'll be in touch and thanks very much.'

'They've accepted the offer!' she said, clapping her hands together.

'Great,' I said, 'That means we want a mortgage of only twenty thousand, I'll go to the building society as soon as I've picked up the negs from the art studio.

I jumped into the car and went to pick up the negatives from the art and design studio, paid the director £20 and went on to the building society. There I met a financial assistant who wanted to know how much I earned, I told a lie and said I was earning £500 a week from the printing business.

'I don't think you're mortgage will be a problem Richard,' he said in a friendly way.

"OK, then, get me all mortgaged up,' I said.

'Right,' he replied, 'I'll make all the arrangements.'

After a bit of form filling I was mortgaged to the tune of twenty grand. I decided to call on Reg.

'Hi,' I said as he opened the door, 'Just thought I'd pay you a visit to see how you're going on.'

"Oh, great,' he said ushering me in, 'The cheques have arrived. That means I owe you a few quid. Here, I'll write you a cheque right away.' Reg wrote me a cheque for £800.

'Ooh, ta,' I said, 'We'll soon have that piddling little mortgage paid off at this rate!' I thought.

'You'll never guess what Dick,' said Reg excitedly. 'New Scientist want me to write an article for them, and the BBC want me to do Horizon. And, oh yes, I've finished the paper for Nature, Marcia's going to get her secretary to type it up for me.'

"I reckon that's a grand for the New Scientist article and five thou for Horizon, after all it is nationwide, although I don't know how much to charge Nature. I suppose it's a prestige thing with them so we'll wait and see if they pay anything.' I said rubbing my hands together. 'Let's have a drink to celebrate. Oh, and you should get yourself a laptop.'

Reg got two cans of Boddies from the fridge and actually offered me one! Mind you, he could well afford it now. 'How did you get on with Marcia the other night?' I asked.

'Oh, great, she loved the takeaway and Forest Gump on the tele, she hadn't seen it you know.'

After a good glug and some friendly backslapping I left Reg to his own devices and went home.

I went into the garage with the negs and made up the first two of four printing plates to do Henri Boyds letterheads. It took me the rest of the day to run the job off. Prue typed up the invoice after I'd finished.

That night I went into the garage, took a deep breath and thought about the scum that was terrorizing the neighbourhood on the local council estate, 'I don't suppose it will do any harm to go take a look see,' I thought.

I believed in Reg's theory I thought, then I thought of the council estate where the problem family lived, the garage began to glow blue and I disappeared to materialize outside a row of semi-detached houses with neat gardens. It didn't take me long to suss out which house held the retard family, the garden was littered with rubbish and an old bike frame and a useless fridge. The two yobs were in next door's garden, one frozen in the act of throwing some dog shit in a plastic bag at the front door.

'Dirty little bastard,' I thought. I walked up to them and thought long and hard, anger filling me up. I struck the one with the dog shit on the side of the head, his head immediately burst into fragments, and then, sod it, I struck the other one too. There was now two headless retards standing there. 'We'll see what your mother has to say about that, then,' I thought. Immediately I willed myself back into my garage.

I was trembling with excitement, I had actually done it! Let that be a lesson to all retards!

Well that took care of Monday. In the evening of the Tuesday I took a stroll down to the local newsagents and bought a copy of the local newspaper. The headline blared: TWO MORE HEADLESS BODIES FOUND ON LOCAL ESTATE.

The following article read:

Two more headless bodies were found by a local couple on the driveway of their house last night. They had both what is described by police as 'severe trauma' to the head, the police are linking it to the case of the headless corpse found in Humber Street. Both cases are exactly alike.

When I got in Prue said, 'The estate agents have been on the phone to see if we'd like to view the bungalow, so I've made arrangements for tomorrow.'

'That'll be fine. Perhaps we can stop for a pub grub on the way down there,' I replied.

"Ooh, yes that would be great.'

CHAPTER 13

The next day saw us on the way to Wales, we stopped off in Chester for a lunch of fish and chips in an Olde World pub and by two we were outside the estate agents. The agent turned out to be a rather portly chap with a sunny disposition. 'I'll take you down to the bungalow in my car,' he said, 'just a mo, I'll get the keys.

After about fifteen minutes we were outside the bungalow. The agent ushered us in. In the hall there was the unmistakable outline of the grandfather clock that we had seen when looking through the letterbox. The kitchen comprised of a couple of scruffy base units and an old Belfast sink, it would need a new fitted kitchen, 'Never thought of that did we,' I muttered to Prue.

'Well, a couple of grand should put it right,' she replied brightly.

The bedrooms were at the back of the bungalow and were adequate for our needs being of average size, they both had open fireplaces. The lounge had a wood burning stove in it. 'Just look at that fireplace,' said Prue, 'Isn't it to die for?' The floorboards were in excellent condition, hidden under the linoleum. There was a master bedroom in the roof space upstairs.

'Yeah, it is, I said thinking of how I was to get rid of all the distemper on the walls. The garden at the back, like the

front, was overgrown with weeds. 'This will take some work,'
I said.

'Well, I love it,' said Prue, 'I can just imagine us living here.'

'OK, then we'll see the solicitor tomorrow,' I replied. 'Ooh,
can we?' she said with a big smile on her face.

When we were on our way home I switched on the portable
radio to catch the news, it was dominated by the case of the
two headless louts found the day before yesterday and about
how the police were clueless as to what had happened.

Meanwhile at the police station DI Harrison was talking to
the forensic technician and the police psychologist.

"If you ask me it was the same murderer who did both
crimes, they are identical in nature, massive trauma to the
head, but what was the murder weapon? We haven't got a
clue.'

The psychologist said, 'I think we have a vigilante out there,
a loner. After all, these lads were no angels were they? They
were all up to no good when they met their deaths.'

'I'm arranging for all my officers to interview all the neighbours
in the area and I want that Percy in for questioning. I believe
he had a run in with one of the lads,' said DI Harrison.

The next day I went round to the solicitors and left all details
of the bungalow and the estate agents etc. I left one of my
business cards in case he wanted any stationery. When I
got home there was some mail, one of the letters contained

a cheque from Henri Boyds for their stationery, I was dead chuffed with it. There was a knock on the front door. I looked through the window, it was a police officer! My mouth went dry. I answered the door.

'Good afternoon sir, just a few questions. Where were you on the 13th of this month?'

'I was in the garage,' I replied.

'Have you had any trouble with vandals around here?'

"No officer, it's pretty quiet around here,' I said.

'Have you seen anybody running away or anybody with blood on them?'

"No certainly not officer, have you any idea of who did the murders?'

"To be quite honest sir, we don't have a clue, right, we'll try your next door neighbour, thanks for your co-operation sir.'

"Goodbye, officer.'

I walked down to the newsagents and ordered a copy of 'Nature' I had to read Reg's paper didn't I?

When I got home the phone rang, it was Reg, 'Can you run me down to the BBC tomorrow Dick, they want to start the filming of Horizon.'

'Sure I can Mate," I replied, after all I had nothing on for the next day.

'Right, see you tomorrow Dick,' said Reg and he rang off.

I thought about where to transport myself to that night, no, no more murders I promised myself. I know, what about the moon! After tea I slipped away into the garage, I thought of Reg's theory and how much I believed in it then thought about the sea of tranquility on the moon. A wave of blue light diffused over me and I disappeared to materialize on the lunar surface in the crater of the sea of tranquility. The great ball of the earth hung in the sky illuminating the grey brown surface of the moon, I looked into the near distance, I could see the base of the Lunar Module first used by the astronauts in1969! There was an American flag, frozen nearby, I loped up towards the LM, the feeling of lower gravity was exhilarating. And there before me was the footprints of Neil Armstrong and 'Buzz' Aldrin as fresh as they were on 20.17. July 1969, after they had been transported here by Apollo 11! So it wasn't a hoax after all, they had really walked on the moon. That was one in the eye for all the doubters out there. I just stood in wonderment at the scene before me, the horizon seemed nearer than it actually was due to the absence of air on the moon. I spent half an hour investigating my surroundings before thinking of my garage and re-appearing there.

When I got indoors Prue was sat down watching television. 'There's a programmeme on tonight, Dick. It's right up your street about quantum mechanics. And there's another one about The Gooch Street Gang in Moss Side.'

'Oh, that's interesting,' I said pouring myself a whiskey and tonic, 'Do you want one love? I'm taking Reg to the BBC studios tomorrow.' I was still exhilarated about my recent trip to the moon.

I sat down in the armchair to watch the television, the programme about quantum mechanics was interesting, then the programme about the Gooch Street gang started. It was about how they lived their drug-filled lives, living off protection rackets and selling cocaine, they caused a lot of people a lot of misery. 'Hmm, perhaps they needed some of my attention,' I thought. Soon it was time for bed. I dreamt I was flying to the moon. Soon the alarm went off and it was time to get up. After a shower and shave I breakfasted and then went round to Reg's.

CHAPTER 14

I knocked on his door three times before a dozy Reg answered in his pajamas. 'Come on Reg,' I said, 'this is one of the most important days of your life, you will be seen nationwide, not to mention other countries in the program where you appear.'

'I'm knackered,' said Reg, 'It's Marcia's fault, she's insatiable.'

'So you got it on then did you?' I replied.

'Sure did man, sure did.'

'Guess where I visited last night, Reg.'

'Go on, tell me,' said Reg.

"Tranquility base on the moon. I saw the lunar module and the astronauts' footprints and everything.'

'Been there myself," Reg replied. 'It's awe inspiring isn't it?'

'Did you see that program on quantum mechanics last night,' I asked.

'Yeah,' he replied, 'not enough maths for me though.'

Soon we were on our way towards the BBC television studios in Manchester. When we got there we were introduced to the producer, Bill Davidson.

'Before we go on,' I said, 'Reg's appearance fee is £5000.'

'Yes, that will be OK,' said Davidson straight away.' 'Oh, and please call me Bill.'

'Heck,' I thought, 'maybe we should have asked for more.'

'What we're going to be doing today is all the parts of the program where you appear in it then we add all the illustration work and special effects later on,' said Bill.

The filming took all day, Reg was a natural, he took it all in his stride and was completely at home in the studio. What a difference from the shy reclusive man he once was.

Soon it was time for home. I bought a newspaper on the way, there was nothing relating to the murders, just an article on some MP who was fiddling his expenses.

'Is Marcia coming round tonight, Reg?'

'She is, yes.' God, they were inseparable.

I dropped Reg off at his house and called on Percy. 'I've just come to see how you are,' I said as he answered the door.

'Oh, I'm fine,' he said. 'It's been absolute heaven and quiet ever since that dickhead got his head kicked in. The police took me in for questioning, you know, honestly as if I had the energy to do that, I'm ninety years old!

'See you then Percy.' I got in the car and went home, thinking about The Gooch Street Gang.

That night I returned to the garage and did the usual thing to dematerialize, I thought of the pub where the gang were most likely to be, The Grapes in Moss Side. Sure enough I appeared in the main lounge of the pub which was quite crowded, punters stood and sat around, frozen in various poses of drinking, chatting and so on. There was a quite attractive girl behind the bar. I strolled across the room to a door marked PRIVATE and entered. Jackpot! There were eight of them there in their own private lounge. They were all smoking Ganja and sprawled around in various poses. Without hesitating I ambled up to the nearest gangster and shattered his head, then the next one and the next. I did seven of them and left the eighth to tell the tale. I willed myself back into my garage.

Seen from Four dimensional space time the remaining gangster saw his companions' heads exploding one at a time, he was shocked to the core and screamed like a baby. 'My God, My Holy God. What's happening? They're all dead.' He ran out of the room and into the main lounge still babbling and wailing Some of the bystanders went into the private room to take a look see. 'Christ, it's a blood bath!' said one. Somebody phoned the police and ambulance service.

After about 15 minutes the police arrived followed by the ambulance men. The police were from Manchester, they got on their radio and requested a senior officer, about 10 minutes later a Detective Inspector arrived who surveyed the scene of the crime. 'Hell,' he said, 'what the fuck's happened here, I've never seen anything like it in my whole life.' He turned toward the assembled crowd, 'OK, who saw what happened?'

'Me,' said the remaining gangster.

'Do tell,' said the DI.

Hysterically the gangster said, 'Man, we were just sitting there having a little smoke and takin' it easy when, all of a sudden, their heads blew up, one by one. Who's done it man?'

'I haven't got a clue, mate,' said the DI.

The following morning I did my usual and bought a morning paper. The headline read: ENTIRE GANG MURDERED. The article read:

The entire members of the infamous Gooch Street gang were found murdered in The Grapes public house in Moss Side last night. The one remaining member of the gang who witnessed the attack said that their heads just blew up one by one. The police have stated that the act was a carbon copy of the murders of three youths the other week.

The headline of another read: VIGILANTE OR ACT OF GOD?

The article read:

*Church leaders were speculating on the bizarre murders of
The Gooch Street gang and the three troublemakers today.
Saying that Divine Intervention could be the cause of death
as the victims were all 'scum' or else a determined vigilante
was on the loose in the area.*

I smiled as I read the articles. I suppose it could be construed
as the wrath of God couldn't it?

A month passed by and the police were still barking up the
wrong tree. Figures released by the Crime Statistics Unit
revealed that acts of public nuisance and crime in general
had fallen by some seventy percent since the murders took
place. 'Result!' I thought. The murders were brought up in
Parliament. One Tory MP said, 'It was good riddance to bad
rubbish!'

A couple of days later Prue and I were called to the solicitor's
office and told that we were now the proud owners of the
bungalow. The printing business was going from strength to
strength and I started to get repeat orders.

CHAPTER 15

I began refurbishing the bungalow. I started by ripping up all the tatty linoleum to reveal pristine floorboards underneath. I hired a sanding machine and got to work. I was interrupted periodically by the printing, but there was no rush. I then sanded all the paintwork and primed it, then I washed down all the walls with sugar soap and painted plaster stabilizer on them from B&Q. The walls were in excellent condition and would only need emulsioning, which I was glad about.

One day when I was working on the bungalow Prue drove up all excited. 'Look what I've bought for the hallway.' she said gleefully. She revealed in the boot, a full-sized grandfather clock in perfect working order. 'I got it from the auctioneer's in Eccles,' she said. We both carried it in and positioned it where the previous owner's clock had stood. I attached the pendulum to it and it began to tick away merrily, it chimed on the hour and on the half-hour.

Soon it was time to paint the walls, we decided on cream for the walls and white for the paintwork, done in a silk paint. I took all the interior doors off and had them stripped in Chester and then I varnished them. We got a local firm to fit a new kitchen for three and a half grand. But we kept the Belfast sink. Soon it was time to furnish the house, it cost us an arm and a leg to buy a bed, three piece suite and some second-hand pine wardrobes. We didn't need a washing machine because the one at home would be used for all the washing. We also bought rugs to go on the floors. The kitchen floor was tiled in the original slate flooring.

Reg had his paper published in 'Nature' but it was too complicated for me what with all the equations, etc. The article in New Scientist was far more readable. Reg was called upon to lecture at The Manchester Astronomical Society and even at Cambridge, soon America and Japan were calling for his services. He had even written an article for Playboy magazine.

This morning I bought the Telegraph it contained an article which read:

Above a calm, dark ocean, a huge, bloated red sun rises in the sky—a full ten times the size of our sun as seen from earth. Small waves lap at a sandy shore and on the beach, something stirs . . . .

This is the scene—or may be the scene—on what is possibly the most extraordinary world to have been found outside our Solar System.

The discovery was announced today by a team of European astronomers, using a telescope in La Silla in the Chilean Andes.

The earth-like planet, that could be covered in oceans and may support life is 20.5 light years away, and has the right temperature to allow liquid water on its surface.

This remarkable discovery appears to confirm the suspicions of most astronomers that the universe is swarming with earth-like worlds.

We don't yet know much about this planet, but scientists believe that it may be the best candidate so far for supporting extraterrestrial life.

The new planet, which orbits a small, red star called Gliese 581, is about one-and-a-half times the diameter of the earth.

It probably has a substantial atmosphere and may be covered with large amounts of water-necessary for life to evolve—and, most importantly, temperatures are very similar to those on our own world.

It is the first exoplanet (a planet orbiting a star other than our Sun) that is anything like our Earth.

Of the 220 or so exoplanets found to date, most have either been too big, made of gas rather than solid material, far too hot, or far too cold for life to survive.

'On the treasure map of the Universe, one would be tempted to mark this planet with an X,' says Xavier Delfosse, one of the scientists who discovered the planet. 'Because of its temperature and relative proximity, this planet will probably be a very important target of the future space missions dedicated to the search for extraterrestrial life.'

Gliese 581 is among the closest stars to us, just 20.5 light years away (about 120 trillion miles) in the constellation Libra. It is so dim it can only be seen with a good telescope.

Because all planets are relatively so small and the light they give off so faint compared to their sun, finding exoplanets is extremely difficult unless they are huge.

According to Seth Shostak, of the Search for Extraterrestrial Intelligence Institute in California, the Gliese system is now a prime target for a radio search.

'We had actually looked at this system before but only for a few minutes. We heard nothing, but now we must look again.'

By 2020 at least one space telescope should be in orbit, with the capability of detecting signs of life on planets orbiting nearby stars. If oxygen or methane (tell-tale biological gases) are found in Gliese 581's atmosphere, this would be good circumstantial evidence for life.

Dr. Malcolm Fridlund, a European Space Agency scientist, said the discovery of Gliese 581c was an 'important step' on the road to finding life.

'If this is a rocky planet, it's very likely it will have liquid water on its surface, which means there may also be life.'

Such as The real importance is not so much the discovery of this planet itself, but the fact that it shows that Earth-like planets are probably extremely common in the Universe.

There are 200 billion stars in our Galaxy alone and many astronomers believe most of these stars have planets.

The fact that almost as soon as we have built a telescope capable of detecting small Earth-like worlds, one turns up right on our cosmic doorstep, shows that statistically, there are probably billions of Earths out there.

As Seth Shostak says: 'We've never found one close to being like the Earth until now. We are finding that Earth is not such an unusual puppy in the litter of planets.'

But are these alien Earths home to life? No one knows. We don't understand how life began on our world, let alone how it could arise anywhere else.

There may be an awful lot of bugs and bacteria out there, and only a few worlds with what we would recognise as plants and animals. Or, of course, there may be nothing.

The Search for Extraterrestrial Intelligence Institute uses radio telescopes to try to pick up messages sent by alien civilisations.

Interestingly, Gliese 581c is so close to the Earth that if its putative inhabitants only had our level of technology, they could—just about—pick up some of our radio signals, such as the most powerful military transmitters. Quite what would happen if we for our part did receive a signal is unclear.

'There is a protocol, buried away in the United Nations,' says Dr. Shostak. 'The President would be told first, after the signal was confirmed by other observatories. But we couldn't keep such a discovery secret.'

It may be some time before we detect any such signals, but it is just possible that today we are closer than ever to finding life in the stars.

'That's the great debate,' I thought. 'Is there life in the Universe. Well, there was only one way to find out, I had to visit Gliese 581c myself.

CHAPTER 16

That night saw me in my garage, thinking hard about the Gliese system, this was seriously far away from home. I disappeared into the blue light and reappeared looking down on the exoplanet. I felt like the star child in the film 2001. Yes, there were oceans down there and land masses, too. The planet had two polar caps and what appeared to be vegetation! I landed on a beach of grey volcanic sand lined by huge tropical-type trees. There were waves on the sea, frozen in space and time. I felt elated, there has to be life here I thought to myself. I walked up to the tree-line.

And, of my God, there in amongst the shrubbery was an armadillo-type creature, and looking up into the trees were bat-like birds. I pushed on and struggled through the exotic foliage, and came face-to-face with a huge creature resembling a tiger, caught in the act of stalking its prey.

I struggled on and came to a clearing and there, to my amazement, were structures rising up from the ground, they were buildings of some sort. In among the structures were strange three-legged creatures with small metallic bodies and transparent domes covering their heads, inside each dome was the head, of what can only be described, as that of an ant Then it hit me, the alien life form was part organic and part machine! In the centre of the clearing was a domed building, I walked up to it breathing heavily as the gravity on this planet was twice that of Earth. I peered through an opening the size of an average doorway, inside in neat rows were eggs ready for hatching just like an ant's nest on Earth.

Strange symbols were painted on the walls and in the centre of the dome, about the size of a car was what appeared to be a computer console with an illuminated screen.

So here the debate ended, there was intelligent life other than on Earth in the universe. The pity was that only myself and Reg would ever know about it. I stayed for approximately half an hour soaking up the wonderful panorama of diverse life that this planet displayed, but I was getting winded by the 2 times gravity. Looking up I saw the pale shape of one of the planet's moons, so I decided to transport myself there. The moon was heavily cratered just like Earth's moon, but on its surface there were dome-like structures, transparent and inside were more ant-creatures. So they were intelligent enough to colonise their moon I thought.

I felt the urge to tell someone this fabulous story but who would believe me? They would think I was some kind of basket case. I transported myself back to my garage.

When I got indoors Prue was there, 'where have you been?' she retorted, 'I've been looking all over for you.'

'Oh, I was just out for a walk, love,' I lied.

'There's been a chap on the phone who owns an auction house he wants 20,000 leaflets, A4 as soon as possible. I took his address and told him you'd see him tomorrow.'

'Ah, you did well, Chuck,' I replied. I went into the lounge and settled down in front of the television, not really seeing it, as my mind was in a whirl thinking of all the wondrous things I had seen. I went to bed and dreamt I was being chased by huge flesh eating ants.

The next day I called in at the auctioneer's show rooms, he gave me a rough proof of what he wanted, and he was pleased when I told him I would deliver the day after tomorrow. I took the proof to the art house for typesetting and negative to make the printing plate, they said that they could do it that day, which was good because I could run the job off the next day and deliver the day after. Here I was printing 'money' again.

I was thinking of what I was capable of and of how I could put it to good use, to help someone out, you know what I mean, dear reader?

My attention was drawn to an article on Robert Mugabe in a magazine, it read:

When Robert Mugabe came to power in 1980 the talk was of peace and co-operation after decades of white colonial rule and bitter civil war.

Taking the helm of the newly renamed nation of Zimbabwe he was quickly elevated to the ranks of international statesman.

He has, however, always been regarded as something of a political enigma.

Raised and educated as a Roman-Catholic Mr. Mugabe became a committed Marxist during the guerrilla war against the Rhodesian Front government of Ian Smith.

Taking power on a wave of popular support his early political promises of reconciliation and democracy were later overtaken by a strong authoritarian streak and a deep distrust of opposition.

Born in 1924, Robert Gabriel Mugabe was educated in missionary schools and received the first of his seven degrees from South Africa's Fort Hare University.

Returning to Rhodesia in 1960 he joined Joshua Nkomo's Zimbabwe African People's Union (Zapu) but left three years later to form the rival Zimbabwe African National Union (Zanu).

Jailed without trial for 10 years he left Rhodesia for neighbouring Mozambique in 1974 and led the largest of the guerrilla forces fighting a protracted and bloody war against the Smith government.

After months of negotiations the 1979 Lancaster House agreement set the seal on a Rhodesian peace deal and Mr. Mugabe returned home to a rapturous welcome from black supporters.

He initially built a coalition government with Mr. Nkomo, Whose Zapu forces had also fought the Smith government, but the discovery of a large arms cache at Zapu-owned houses led to Mr. Nkomo's dismissal from government.

A brutal crackdown on Zapu supporters followed, leading many commentators to compare Mr. Mugabe's own approach to political opposition with that during the time of white rule.

The collapse of the coalition allowed Mr. Mugabe to strengthen his hold on power.

In recent years Mr. Mugabe has become an increasingly outspoken nationalist, lashing out at the 75,000 white Zimbabweans and their alleged foreign backers for his country's economic collapse.

Mr. Mugabe has made much of his devout Christianity, but his marriage to a former private secretary in 1996—41 years his junior and with whom he already fathered two children—raised more than a few eyebrows.

At the same time he has persued what he regards as a deeply moral campaign against homosexuality making 'unnatural sex acts' illegal with a penalty of **up to 10 years in prison**.

A vocal opponent of colonialism Mr. Mugabe has been criticised for committing his armed forces to what many see as little more than a wasteful colonial-style intervention in the Congolese civil war.

*The war has also raised accusations of corruption, with government officials alleged to **be lining their pockets from Congo's rich mineral reserves while Zimbabwe's own economy plummets out of control.***

*Local journalists who have tried to investigate these and other allegations against Mr. Mugabe and his family say they have been **intimidated and in some cases tortured.***

Until recently, Mr. Mugabe had always been able to stifle political opposition. His Zanu-PF party still dominates what is virtually a one party state occupying 147 out of the country's 150 parliamentary seats.

Growing discontent over the country's failing economy with inflation and unemployment soaring to record levels are starting to threaten his authority.

And with defeat for President Mugabe in the constitutional referendum, his long stated aim of handing over large tracts of fertile land from whites to blacks looks no nearer to being resolved.

The issue, which was a major cause of the guerrilla war for independence in the 1970s, looks likely to remain mired in arguments over compensation.

So there we have it, what we've got here is a tyrant who tortures his own people and who steals land and farms from the white population while his cronies pocket money and his own economy plummets out of control leading to misery for the population of Zimbabwe. All the while clinging on to power by rigging the elections and intimidating his own people. It was high time that Mr. Mugabe was taught a lesson.

I went round to the art studio that day and picked up the negative for the print job, the next day I ran it off and parcelled up the leaflets ready for delivery and placed them in the boot of the Metro. The day after that I delivered them to a delighted auctioneer, who paid up promptly. 'I will be wanting these every month,' he said.

'Only too glad to be of service,' I replied.

The next day I had nothing to do so Prue and I decided to go to the bungalow for a few days, we left the phone on answer machine in case we had any print enquiries. It was too much of a risk to dematerialise myself at the bungalow so I gave it no more thought. That was until we got back home.

I went into the garage in the evening under the pretext of doing some machine maintenance: I thought of the theory and then of Mugabe's house in Zimbabwe, the garage glowed its usual blue (I must ask Reg why this happens I thought) I dematerialised and appeared outside a beautiful colonial styled house. I entered through the front door, the house was deserted. There was a light coming from under the stairs. I walked over towards it and realised that there were some steps that led to a cellar, I descended the stairs, when I got to the basement I was confronted by a diabolical scene: Mugabe and one of his henchmen (nicknamed Hitler because he had forced one of the white farmers to drink diesel) were standing facing some poor sod tied to a chair. His face was contorted in pain and there was blood and snot everywhere, they had really given the bloke a good pasting. I walked casually in a circle round the two thugs, the henchman had a vicious looking knuckleduster on his right hand. I went up to him and smashed him in the head with a right hook. His head burst into blood red fragments. I circled Mugabe and held his hand, I took hold of his ring finger and snapped it off like a dry twig. Then I unbuttoned the top pocket of his safari jacket and popped a note in it, it read:

You'd better call a fair election next week or the same will happen to you, you have been warned.

Seen from Mugabe's point of view he saw 'Hitlers' head explode and his finger inexplicably sever from his hand 'Oh, God help me, it hurts, it hurts.' He cried out in agony. Another of his henchmen came running in 'What's up boss, what happened?' he looked on in horror at his decapitated partner, then he checked on the prisoner. No, it couldn't be him, he was still tied firmly to the chair.

'Voodoo,' screamed the henchman, 'It must be the work of a witch!'

'Nonsense,' said Mugabe, 'get me a doctor, my hand is killing me.' There was blood all over his safari suit.

'Black magic' screamed the hysterical thug.

Mugabe then noticed the note in his pocket, he took it out and read it, he started to shake.

About half an hour went past and eventually a doctor arrived to dress Mugabe's hand.

A week later Mugabe went to the country and held an election, he lost and the opposition swept in with a landslide vote, his bandaged hand was there for everyone to see, he blamed it on 'a gardening accident.' His own state police could find no cause for the attack, they were completely baffled as to the Perpetrator of the crime.

CHAPTER 17

It was a Saturday and I decided to call on Reg, but Marcia was there as usual.

'I've got some news,' said Reg, 'Marcia and me, we're going to get married in six months time!'

'Oh, congratulations,' I replied, 'you will be well suited,' I lied. Scruffy Reg and posh Marcia, an unlikely couple, I thought. Ah, well they say opposites attract don't they?

Reg was now earning tens of thousands from articles and public appearances, he was still giving me my 20 percent, as I was arranging all of his bookings, he might as well cash in now because I can't see it lasting I thought. After some small talk I decided to leave and let Marcia and Reg alone.

I stood in Reg's doorway.

'There's something I've been meaning to ask you, Reg,' I said as I was going. 'Why does everything go blue when we're dematerialising?'

'Oh, that,' he replied. 'It's a shockwave, a blue shift, it's caused by the atoms of your body slowing down to absolute relative rest. It's the opposite of the red shift that you see in the universe when galaxies are speeding away from you.'

'Right,' I said. I still found it hard to fathom out, but I still had to believe in Reg's theory or I wouldn't be able to transpose myself.

The next week went by without incident, I had two print jobs to do that would earn me over £400. Which wasn't bad.

The police had a visitor, a member of M15, agent Rothwell, to meet DI Harrison. The two men were deep in conversation. There were several members of DI Harrison's team present as well.

DI Harrison began, 'We are still waiting on a lead as to how these people met their deaths. I mean, we have no evidence of what weapon was used and no eyewitness sightings of who the perpetrator was. According to the witness's statements all they saw was the victim's heads spontaneously explode.

Agent Rothwell said, 'I have something here that might interest you and your team,' he revealed a videotape and inserted it into the television. 'It's a CCTV tape taken from President Robert Mugabe's house some weeks ago, it was smuggled out of Zimbabwe by one of our agents last week.

The tape began to run, it showed two men facing an unfortunate man tied to a chair, the bloke with Mugabe smacked the victim full in the face with a knuckledustered hand. The man screamed out loud. then just as the thug was about to strike again, all of a sudden, his head burst apart as Mugabe screamed and waves his hand about, one finger clearly missing. Blood and bits of human tissue flew everywhere.

'Well I'll be damned,' exclaimed DI Harrison. 'It's exactly the same as our victims over here, the massive trauma to the head and everything. And it appears that Mugabe lost a finger out of nowhere.'

'Yes,' said agent Rothwell. 'Mugabe tried to make out it was an accident in the garden. And then he takes out a note of some sort from his left jacket pocket that quite clearly, he recoils from in fear. It strikes me as odd that Mubabe called for a general election a week later that was free from the intimidation to his people that he had shown in elections earlier.

'But we're still missing a perpetrator, and there's no weapon evident either, it's as if whoever did it was invisible!'

'That's exactly what my people think, too,' said agent Rothwell. 'Well, I'll leave the tape with you in case you come up with any ideas. We think that the Government science boffins have got a hand in it somewhere and have created an invisibility cloak of some sort. I'll let you know if we come across anything else.' With that he left.

'But we still have no positive leads,' said DI Harrison to his assembled team. 'I think we've got a super vigilante here.' He slumped down at his desk shaking his head in dismay.

CHAPTER 18

As for me I had decided to take the journey of a lifetime.

On a cold clear winter's night if you look up at the sky to the east of the constellation Orion in Taurus the bull you will see the open cluster the Pleiades. You should see seven stars (the seven sisters as the ancients called them) but in fact, there are over 500 stars that make up the open cluster which lies in a gaseous nebula. They are 410 light years distant and comprise of hot B type blue stars which are 100 million years old. I resolved to journey to the largest star Alcyone (eta Tauri).

As usual I was in my garage, Prue was out doing the weekly shop. I thought hard about Alcyone and found myself on the freezing world that was the fourth planet in Alcyone's system. I looked up and the sky was incredible, there were three suns in the sky and countless pinpricks of light which were other suns in the nebula near to the parent star all shining with a hot blue light. It was a sight to behold and I felt privileged to witness it. I was able to roam the system and visited Maia (20 Tauri), Asterope 1&2 (the double star 21 Tauri), Taygeta (21 Tauri), Celaeno (16 Tauri), Electra (17 Tauri) and finally Merope (23 Tauri). A planet was orbiting Merope in the 'goldilocks' area of the system where conditions were right for life to form. I journeyed on to the planet's surface There were flowing waterfalls frozen in space and time and huge oceans, the blue parent star shone in the sky, bathing the planet in just the right amount of radiation, there were no polar caps. As I looked on more closely I saw gentle looking creatures with huge limped eyes and long thin arms and legs sat in boats on the oceans caught in the act of rowing. They were completely naked, with a white translucent skin.

'It seems as though the Universe is teeming with life forms,' I thought. All too soon it was time to go. I had been gone for three hours. I returned to my garage, Prue was still out. I went indoors and sat down in one of the armchairs, I felt elated and full of wonderment over the journey I had just undertaken, I would give my eye teeth to tell someone, but it had to be kept a secret and the only person I could confide in was Reg, and he was too loved up with Marcia to be of any use in a conversation. I resolved to pay him a visit in the near future.

Reg had hit a barren period as far as public appearances were concerned, his theory was now old news and he had published in all the journals and magazines you could shake a stick at.

That night he phoned me up, 'Can you come around tomorrow night Dick?' he said. 'I have put Marcia off for one night, we could have a chin wag like we used to do, and, oh yes, a few tinnies as well. Can you bring some round with you?'

He'd done it again, got me to buy his ale for him yet again, but I didn't mind, it would be great to see him. 'Yes, I'll be glad to come round,' I replied. 'See you about eight.'

"Ok, Ta ta.'

The next day I had a couple of deliveries to make and soon it was time for tea, a good old Lancashire hot-pot. I told Prue I was going round to Reg's that night on 'money matters.' She didn't seem bothered. I decided to walk round to Reg's as it was a lovely evening and besides, I'd be having a drink of alcohol.

I knocked on Reg's front door, he appeared wearing a suit and was clean shaven and smart.

'Wow, get a load of you!' I exclaimed, 'You look proper dapper.'

'Um, I know,' replied Reg, 'it's Marcia, she said I looked too scruffy now that I was in the public eye and it was time to smarten up a bit, so I went to Moss Bros. and bought this, I've even got Calvin Klein underwear on.'

'Well, you look great Reg,' I replied.

I went in and settled in one of Reg's armchairs and cracked open a couple of the cans of Boddies that I had brought with me. After some small talk I was dying to ask Reg a question—'Reg, have you ever encountered alien life forms on your journeys into the fifth dimension?'

'Sure have, pardner,' he said with a benign smile, 'Many times, the whole Galaxy is crawling with 'em. There's some weird and wonderful species out there and places were life has been extinguished like the fifth planet of Betelgeuse for instance. It's now a variable star and wiped out all life on the planet. What's left of the population are now in a spaceship kind of Noah's Ark journeying to a small G type star in Orion in the hope that they will find an hospitable planet there.

'Yes, I have seen life forms too,' I said and told Reg of the strange biological/machine like creatures in the Gliese system.

'Well, I saw an alien life form that was part human and part carbon crystal on a planet rotating round Gamma Cassiopeiae, it's an irregular variable but it still maintains life.'

'We shall have to journey somewhere together sometime,' I said.

'Yes, but not tonight, I'm tired out, anyway, how's Prue and the girls?' said Reg, referring to my two daughters.

'Oh, they're fine, I've got four grandchildren now, three girls and a boy.'

'Talking of family,' said Reg, 'will you be my best man when I get married?'

'I'd be honoured,' I replied. I felt happy that Reg had asked me.

'I have been reading the Guardian today,' said Reg. 'There was an article about Robert Mugabe that had been leaked by m15. Apparently Mugabe's henchman nicknamed 'Hitler' was found decapitated just like those retards over here. Mugabe lost a finger in the attack, he was so traumatized by the incident that he held an intimidation free general election seven days later, the CCTV tape showed no perpetrator of the crime, It's as though he was invisible—I wonder how that could have happened, Dick? Reg stared at me fixedly.

'I, I don't know, it's a mystery to me,' I lied. Anything can happen these days what with modern technology and stuff.'

I could feel my cheeks starting to flush bright red.

'Well, just be careful out there then,' said Reg, still staring into my eyes knowingly.

Soon it was 11 o'clock and time to go home, Reg ushered me out and said, 'don't forget to watch your back when you go on your travels.'

'I will. He knows," I thought.

I took a slow stroll home, deep in thought, I heeded Reg's warning but I couldn't give it up could I? There were still dictators and despots out there like Muammar Gaddafi and Osama Bin Laden to name but two.

CHAPTER 19

The next day we were on our way to the bungalow after making a stationery delivery to a double glazing company on the way. When we got there we decided to spend the day working in the garden. There was still plenty to do like weeding and pruning, etc.

I soon got a thirst on as the sun was shining brightly, so I went into the kitchen to get a couple of beers, 'Do you want a beer, Chuck?' I shouted to Prue. Who was tackling the overgrown ivy on the fencing which surrounded the garden.

'Love one,' came her reply.

When I got into the kitchen a strange sight was waiting for me, all the kitchen cupboard doors and drawers were open and pulled out.

'What the . . . ?' I thought.

I closed all the cupboard doors and shut the drawers. I went to the fridge and got two ice cold beers out. I went outside to Prue.

'Have you been rooting around in the kitchen?' I asked.

'No. What would I want in there?'

'It's just that all the cupboard doors were wide open and all the drawers were pulled out,' I said.

'On, that'll be him again.'

'Who's him?' I asked.

'Why, the previous owner of course.'

'Nonsense,' I replied, 'he's as dead as a doornail.'

'Yeah, I know.'

'Are you saying that a dead man has been rifling through our kitchen?' I retorted.

'I certainly am.'

'Are you saying we've got a ghost, then.'

'Yup.'

I couldn't believe how unfazed Prue was about the situation. Anyway I didn't believe her, it was crazy and I don't believe in the undead.

We both carried on working in the garden until the sun was going down.

'I'm starving,' I said, 'I'll make the tea tonight. I'll rustle up a couple of mushroom omelets.' I went into the kitchen through the side door. Goddam it, all the kitchen unit doors were wide open and all the drawers were pulled out again!

'If this is Prue's idea of a joke . . . .' I thought. I shut all the doors and pushed the drawers to. I got some eggs out of the fridge and some mushrooms and started to prepare our meal.

While eating I said to Prue, 'Have you seen this so-called ghost then, Chuck!'

'A few times.'

'Where?' I replied.

'In the hallway near the grandfather clock.'

'I don't believe this,' I retorted, 'There's no such thing as ghosts.'

But then I thought of my own experiences as I roamed the Universe, I was like a ghost, visiting all those places without being seen or heard wasn't I?

Prue said, 'Do you know when I bought the grandfather clock? Well, I was buying it for him because he needs it.'

'D'you mean to say that you actually bought a ghost a present!' I exclaimed.

'Well, not exactly, it was for us as well.'

'Oh, that was nice of you,' I said sarcastically. 'Are you sure it wasn't you that opened all the cupboards and drawers?'

'On my kids life.'

Prue would never swear on the girls life if it wasn't true.

That night I couldn't sleep, having a ghost in the house was unnerving me no end. I decided to go down to the kitchen and make a brew. I was halfway down the stairs when I heard a male voice humming, 'It's a Long Way to Tipperary, It's a Long Way to Go.' I went through the kitchen and into the hall, the humming stopped, there was nothing there. I thought for a moment and returnec to the kitchen. Then I realised what I must do, I thought of the theory and how much I believed in it and then of the hallway, I then appeared right next to the grandfather clock. To my surprise there was the figure of a man clothed in a dressing gown and he was frozen in the act of winding up the clock!

'Gotcha!' I thought to myself, I put out my hand to touch the figure but my hand went straight through him, the figure promptly disappeared. 'So that's our ghost then is it?' I thought.

I materialised back into the kitchen, slightly shaken, what with alien life forms and now ghosts it was all getting a bit much. I brewed up and sat down in the kitchen to reflect on what I had just witnessed, sipping the steaming tea. Perhaps ghosts are aliens?

I went up the stairs slowly, ears pricked, but there was no sound coming from the hallway. I went back to bed and slept fitfully, I resolved to find out a bit more about our ghost.

CHAPTER 20

I got up the next morning early, Prue was fast asleep, I went down to the kitchen—All the chairs were stacked neatly on top of the large farmhouse table! I returned them to where they should be and went into the hall, and went immediately back into the kitchen—the chairs were back on the table! I was in a state of shock and could feel my pulse accelerate, this ruled out the remotest chance that it was Prue.

I made some toast and brewed up, taking some breakfast in for Prue in bed.

'What have I done to deserve this?' she said sleepily.

'Oh, I couldn't sleep so I thought I'd treat you to breakfast in bed.'

I explained to Prue what had happened in the kitchen, 'I'm just letting you know that I believe your ghost story. So I'm gonna take a walk down to the pub after dinner because I want to ask the locals about the man who used to live here. Want to come?'

'This should be interesting,' said Prue Matter-of-factly.

So, after dinner saw us taking a leisurely walk on the two-mile journey to the pub, it was a gorgeous day, the sun was shining and the mountains stretched into the blue haze, I realised then that this was the reason we moved here, for days like this. Soon we were at the pub. I went inside and was greeted by the landlord with a 'hello, son, what can I get you?'

'Two halves of bitter please,' I replied, 'Actually, there was something you can help me with I hope.'

'Oh, what's that then,' said the landlord, pulling the beer, 'There, take a sip.'

I took a good mouthful of the ale and the landlord promptly refilled the glass, as usual there was a group of locals sat in the corner, I nodded towards them, 'hiya,' said one. Prue entered the room.

I said 'you know we've moved into the bungalow down the lane don't you?'

'Yes, I do,' said the landlord.

'Well, I thought you might be able to tell my wife and I about the previous occupant, I understand it was a man on his own.'

The landlord and locals immediately began talking to each other in Welsh. Then one of the locals piped up, 'That would be Dennis Giles. He was about sixty when he died.'

The group chatted again, then the landlord said, 'He lived there with his wife, Mabel, they were very close to each other, unfortunately she died when she was 58, of liver cancer, Dennis never got over it and he committed suicide. His nephew found him hanging from the stair rail at the end of a rope. Why do you ask?'

I explained to them the events that had led up to the ghostly happenings.

'Seems like you've got one humdinger of a ghost there,' said one of the lads.

We came out of the pub and took a leisurely stroll back to the bungalow deep in conversation, 'How often have you seen our 'visitor' then?' I asked Prue.

'Oh everyday,' she replied.

'Aren't you scared?'

'No, not at all.'

We got back to the bungalow in time for tea, when we let ourselves in, the grandfather clock had been moved to the middle of the hall! 'We're gonna have to do something about this,' I said as I moved the clock back into place.

But what?

The next day saw us on our way home. I had some printing to do and our daughters were coming to visit. The following day I finished printing and went to the library, I browsed through the books in the reference section until I came to one called 'Supernatural Phenomena and Exorcism.' I decided to borrow it.

I read through the book from cover to cover especially the part on exorcism.

I was sat in the armchair and Prue was sat on the sofa facing me, 'This book says that a ghost is a poor tortured soul caught in a kind of limbo between this world and the next and the only thing that can release it is to get a priest to perform an exorcism,' I said.

'Well, that should be easy enough. There's a Catholic Church in Betsy Coed. Perhaps we could get help from father what's-his-name there,' Prue replied. 'Poor Dennis is caught between the living and the dead.'

'Oh, were on first name terms with our ghost now!' I shuddered.

We both made up our minds to go to the church the next time we visited the bungalow.

But a visit was out of the question for the moment because the printing was going mad, orders for stationery were coming in from everywhere, and it was Reg's wedding the next weekend.

The next week fairly whizzed by in flurry of printing, making deliveries and a lecture in Birmingham University by Reg. That Saturday I was round at Reg's dressed in my best bib and tucker. The groom looked resplendent in his three piece suit with a flower in the buttonhole. I was a bag of nerves, I took a swig of whiskey from my hip flask that I had brought with me, Reg took a slug too.

All too soon the limo came round to take us to church. As we walked up the aisle to take up our positions I said, 'If you'd have said you'd be getting married a year ago, I would never have believed you. It just goes to show you what can happen in twelve month's time.'

All of a sudden the organ started playing 'Here comes the bride' or the Wedding March or whatever you like to call it, and Marcia entered, looking gorgeous in her white wedding gown with its twelve-foot train, two bridesmaids followed up the rear dressed in wine coloured dresses. Her dad was as proud as Punch.

The service went off without a hitch and soon we were all sat down at dinner in the main banqueting suite at the local variety club. After our meal it was speech time, I started off by telling everybody about Reg's earlier life, and got them all laughing. Among the guests were some celebrities like Beverly Callard from Coronation Street, and a couple from Emmerdale as well.

The reception was great and everybody had a good time getting merry and all that. Soon we were in the taxi bound for home. Reg and Marcia left at about 12 p.m. to go to the airport and then on to Tenerife for their honeymoon.

Two weeks went by and there was a lull in the printing orders, so I took some time out to visit the Catholic Church, Saint Mary's in Betsy Coed, I knocked on the door of the vicarage. The housekeeper answered the door. 'I would like to see Father O'Grady, it's a matter of some importance,' I said to her.

She let me in and said, 'I'll go and see if the Father will see you but you must realise that he's a very busy man.'

After about five minutes a man in his sixties came down the stairs and introduced himself to me. 'I can spare you about fifteen minutes,' said the Father.

We both went into the lounge and got seated, Father O'Grady offered me a whiskey and poured himself one. 'What a nice man,' I thought.

'Now what can I do for you my friend,' he said.

Over the next few minutes I related all the happenings in the bungalow. I included Prue's reactions to the ghost as well.

'Sounds like we're dealing with a poltergeist here and we must perform an exorcism to get rid of it.' said Father O'Grady. 'First I must tell you this: Exorcism has been around for thousands of years, yet it was movies that made it mainstream. To those who've performed this rite, it's not a work of fiction. Exorcisms involve demonic forces with a great deal of power and exorcists with a tremendous amount of faith. Performing an exorcism may take prior training and is often reserved for certain people within a religion, but most rituals follow these steps:

He went on, 'Evaluate your faith. Exorcisms need to be performed by someone with an incredible amount of faith. Most will begin with an appeal to a higher power to commend the poltergeist to leave. Make the sign of the cross at the appropriate times during the prayers. Signing of the cross will be made on both the exorcist (the one performing the rite) as well as the ghost.

Sprinkle holy water on everyone in the room and in the case of Catholic exorcism show the relic of a saint. Again these are all done at the appropriate times during the prayers.

Command the poltergeist out of the house. This will be after the ghost reveals itself. Expect a fight from the ghost. The ghost has found a host and is unwilling to leave quietly. This is a fight for the ghost's soul.'

'Do you think you can help us then, Father?' I asked.

'Yes I think I probably can my son. How about next Wednesday morning, will that suit you?'

'That'll do fine,' I replied. I'll make it do. I thought.

Soon I was back at the bungalow, 'How did you get on,' inquired Prue.

'Oh, all right. The priest's coming round next Wednesday morning, we'll soon have Dennis laid to rest,' I said. From the hall could be heard the strains of 'Pack up your troubles in your old kit bag and smile, smile, smile.'

'Did you hear that?' I asked of Prue. 'Did you hear him singing?'

'Yes I did, he seems quite happy with what we're doing,' said Prue.

'Oh, I'm so glad,' I said with a sarcastic shudder.

CHAPTER 21

Wednesday came around quickly. It was nine a.m. There was a knock on the door of the bungalow. It was Father O'Grady. He entered the hall and then went into the kitchen.

'Hmm, the spirit is strongest in the hall,' he said. He opened his briefcase and took out a religious type of scarf and a crucifix and some holy water in a silver capped bottle. He draped the scarf around his neck and held up the crucifix while splashing the holy water around. He intoned a prayer in Latin, ending with the words 'Be gone oh spirit of this house and lay in eternal rest forever.'

Nothing happened. Father O'Grady carried on with his prayer. In the corner near the window of the hall a faint hint of ectoplasm appeared like smoke it was. Then, 'It's a long way to Tipperary.' The voice appeared to be coming from the corner too. The cloud of ectoplasm took on the shape of a figure of a man although no detail could be seen, just the faint shimmering outline of human form. A voice said 'I think it's time for me to leave now.' The front door flew open and the ectoplasm flowed out through it. The door slammed shut.

'I think we have achieved our goal,' said Father O'Grady. 'It looks as though our spirit has left your house and is laid to rest.

'Thanks a bunch,' I said, 'Do we owe you anything?'

'Just a small donation to the church's roofing fund will suffice,' said Father O'Grady.

I gave him a £20 note, and with that, he left.

'Well, that's that out of the way,' I said to Prue.

'I'm not too sure, Dick, that was far too easy.'

'What do you mean by that?' I said.

'Well, let's just wait and see shall we.' Prue replied.

Prue and I returned to our gardening and the next few days were quiet. It was on the third day when it happened, I was brewing up in the kitchen when I heard the familiar strains of, "It's a long way to Tipperary it's a long way to go . . . .' Well I'll be damned I thought. I went into the hall and there, hanging by the neck from the stair rail was Dennis in all his glory with his eyes bulging out of his sockets!

'Thought you'd got rid of me didn't cha,' he said with a broad toothless grin.

'Jesus,' I said turning away from the apparition. The sight of him was too gruesome to behold. I bolted into the kitchen. One of the kitchen drawers flew open and knives and forks started to fly in all directions. I ran out into the garden.

'Prue, he's back,' I gasped, 'He's hanging from the stair rail.'

'I thought it was too easy to be true,' she said matter-of-factly.

'Come and see,' I said, ashen faced. 'He's just in the hallway.'

We both entered the house together with me gripping Prue's arm. In the kitchen it was quiet save for the cutlery all over the floor, the singing could be heard coming from the hallway. All was normal and there was no sign of the apparition. 'He was here, I swear it,' I gasped, indicating the stair rail.

'I know, I know," said Prue stroking my shoulder, better get on to Father O'Grady and ask for your money back.'

I would have laughed if I wasn't so scared shitless!

That night I was on the phone explaining the day's events to Father O'Grady.

'Well, it seems that we have a determined poltergeist here,' he said, 'Perhaps we need someone with a bit more clout, a bit further up the ecclesiastic ladder, so to speak. I'll get in contact with Archbishop Ryan and see what he can do for you.' He rang off. I poured myself a stiff whiskey.

'What did he say?' asked Prue.

'He's going right to the top, he's enlisting the help of the main man.'

Rick Groves

I poured myself another whiskey and one for Prue. I was soon as pissed as the proverbial fart. When it was time for bed I entered the hallway gingerly. He was there again! Hanging from the stair rail.

'I'm not going anywhere you runt,' said the ghost staring at me with sightless eyes, 'You can get who you want, the Pope even for all I care. Pack All Your Troubles In Your Old Kit Bag And Smile, Smile, Smile . . . .' Then he was silent, nothing could be heard save for the creaking of the rope that he dangled from, then the apparition faded and was gone.

'I saw him again," I said to Prue as she entered the hallway.

'Come on up to bed,' she said from the bottom of the stairs, 'He won't bother you anymore tonight.'

Prue was unfazed by the whole thing, she was as composed as an angel.

I went to the bottom of the stairs, giving the stair rail a wide berth and fairly ran up the stairs.

CHAPTER 22

The next day the phone rang. It was Father O'Grady to say that the Archbishop would visit us on the next day. We stayed out in the garden for the whole of the afternoon, I was too scared to go anywhere near the stairs and hallway. The day went by without a peep from our poltergeist.

We got up to a rainy morning and at nine a.m. there was a knock at the door. It was Father O'Grady accompanied by Archbishop Ryan.

'Good morning, terrible day isn't it?' said Father O'Grady introducing us to the Archbishop.

'I hope you can do something for us Archbishop,' I said, 'the ghost is starting to get more malevolent now.'

'Don't worry my son, I'm sure we can be of assistance.'

Just then a deep growling voice yelled, 'GET OUT OF HERE YOU RUNTS, YOU WON'T GET RID OF ME.' The Archbishop and Father O'Grady were visibly shaken. Then, 'YOU CAN BRING GOD HIMSELF, I AIN'T GOING NOWHERE YOU BASTARDS.'

The Archbishop was dressed in his altar vestments and had a large crucifix on a staff. He also had holy water in a gold-topped bottle, he was armed to the teeth and ready to do battle with the ghost.

The Archbishop intoned something in Latin while holding up the crucifix. The ghost revealed itself hanging from the stair rail, 'OH GOD IT HURTS, IT HURTS,' it growled. The apparition was struggling and kicking out at the end of the rope, hands clutching in vain trying to free itself. All of a sudden the Archbishop was flung off his feet and was thrown against the wall. He faltered in mid prayer but carried on in Latin, something was trying to pull the crucifix from out of his grasp. The apparition began to fade and began to be swallowed up by a cloud of ectoplasm, then, YOU'RE ALL BASTARDS YOU COWARDS, HIDING BEHIND A PRIEST. The voice was weaker now and it faded away as if it was being suffocated out of existence. The Archbishop sprinkled holy water at the ghost as the ectoplasm engulfed it. Father O'Grady was desperately praying hard too. The ectoplasm was fading away and a voice, ever so faint whispered, 'Oh God I'm sorry, I'm sorry. Let me rest, that's all I want is to rest.' Then it was gone.

'Well, I hope that has done the trick,' said the Archbishop smoothing his hair.

'Are you all right?' I asked.

'Just a couple of bruises,' he replied.

'Please let me get you some tea,' said Prue.

We all sat down for a brew in the kitchen and talked of demons, poltergeists and God. Even life in the Universe. Which I was adamant about, of course.

The two gentlemen departed, they had been with us for three hours.

All was quiet. 'Well if that doesn't do it nothing will," I said to Prue. 'We certainly had the big guns at it this time.'

'Yes, he's gone this time,' said Prue washing the teacups.

I felt immensely reassured by what she said.

CHAPTER 23

A fortnight went by and we visited the bungalow twice without incident, the garden was now looking trimmed and tidy, we had worked hard at it. I resolved to invite Reg and Marcia to stay for a weekend. There was at least ten print jobs to do so I got my head down and got stuck in, it took me three days to clear the backlog. I need help I thought. I was friendly with the owner of a large print shop in Trafford Park, so I decided that I would get him to do some jobs for me to take the pressure off for cash in hand of course, so one day I gave them the job for letterheads for a driveway maintenance company called Drive Revive. I picked the job up and paid out £600, delivered it myself and charged £800 to the customer. £200 for half an hours' work, not bad.

Reg was getting less work now but he was still doing OK for himself with the odd lecture and article. Until one day the phone rang, it was Stephen Hawking the world famous physicist's PA! She wanted to arrange a meeting at his convenience up at his house, Hawking would cover Reg's expenses. As soon as I heard the news I went round to Reg's.

'Fancy that,' I said, 'Stephen Hawking the world's greatest mathematician wants to meet you, that's a great honour Reg.'

'Yeah, but I'm scared he might deduce our secret,' said a concerned Reg. 'He's got the mathematical know how to work it out that I fed the other physicists a load of crap.'

'Well, you'll have to meet him, it will seem suspicious if you don't,' I said.

'I know,' aid Reg. He dialed up Hawking's PA and made the arrangements.

I was crapping myself, if our secret got out it would put me right in the frame for the murders that were still unsolved! I could see that Reg was thinking the same thing.

The next day saw us tripping down to London to meet up with Stephen Hawking. It took us four hours to get there to Hawking's Edwardian house. We were shown into a comfortable lounge with a whiteboard and a computer that Hawking could use for communicating with Reg. The great man was wheeled in by his PA. What followed seemed for all intents and purposes like a duel between the two physicists as they sparred with each other, Reg scribbling down formulae like a man possessed, Hawking giving as good as he got on his computer, soon it was time for some refreshments. I didn't have a clue what was going on. The two men carried on discussing Reg's theory as we ate and drank. Then it happened. It came up on Hawking's computer.

'If the fifth dimension does exist as the absolute rest of the Universe then we should be able to transmit matter into it to see if it is viable and that would provide the ultimate proof of the theory.

'Oh my God,' I thought, 'He's on to it,' I looked at Reg, desperation written all over my face.

As cool as a cucumber Reg said, 'Yes, we could but it couldn't be living matter we would have to send a probe of some sort.'

Hawking computed, 'Yes I agree, perhaps NASA could help us there.'

I exhaled in a gasp of relief.

After we had finished and refreshed ourselves, the two men carried on with their mathematical jousting, I heard mention of anti-matter and the Large Hadron Collider and that was where my understanding ended.

Because it was late in the day we were offered a bed for the night in one of the plush bedrooms. We were shown into a large room with two single beds in it. As we got ready for bed I said 'that was a close call Reg, I thought he was going to suss out our secret for sure there.'

'I know, I can't understand how it hasn't been found out, It's so simple it doesn't bear thinking about.'

I fell asleep thinking about the tightrope I was walking.

The next morning we woke to a shower, en suite of course, and a full English breakfast. We said our goodbyes and our thanks and started off for the journey home.

'Have you ever been to the centre of the Galaxy Dick,' said Reg.

'No, I haven't, not yet anyway.'

'You must go, it's truly amazing, there's a large black hole there,' replied Reg.

'I will, soon.'

'I have a place that is so fabulous to visit, but I won't tell you now, it is a place where we shall have to go together,' said Reg mysteriously.

We got home for midday and said our goodbyes.

I went home still thinking with trepidation about the close shave we'd had at Hawking's house. When I got in Prue was doing the washing. 'How'd you get on love,' she enquired.

'Oh great, but I still can't understand it all,' I said.

After tea I went into the garage offering the usual excuse of 'machine maintenance' I thought of the theory then the centre of the Galaxy. The blue shift washed over me, I appeared at the event horizon of the black hole. The black hole event horizon was at least 17 light hours across and was sucking in matter from the nebulae and stars that surrounded it. Fundamental particles were being stripped down into quarks with names like up, down, strange then into tiny coils of 'string' as they disappeared into the singularity. 'This must be the portal to another Universe,' I thought, 'all this matter has to be going somewhere,' I toyed with the idea of entering the black hole itself, but thought better of it. 'What if I couldn't get out.' I thought. I looked around and could see that some of the surrounding stars appeared distorted by the gravitational field of the black hole. And there just outside the event horizon was a machine of some sort with an array of antenna, a probe that had been sent by some intelligence to investigate the black hole, it was fantastic to see. What kind of being had sent it, obviously far superior than mankind was at the moment. It was with great reluctance that I transposed myself back to my garage. 'If these four walls could talk,' I thought.

I went indoors and poured myself a whiskey, Prue was soaking in the bath, my cat DJ jumped up on my knee as I got seated in my favourite armchair. Now worries about being found out receded from my thoughts. I felt euphoric. I made a mental note to ask Reg and Marcia if they would like to visit us at the bungalow at the weekend. I realised that I needed to know what 'string theory' was and resolved to ask Reg next time I saw him.

The next day I phoned Reg to see if he'd like to visit us at the bungalow for the weekend. He seemed quite keen on the idea and he told Marcia there and then, she said she'd be delighted to come. I gave Reg the directions, he said they would arrive in Marcia's car. 'You really must learn to drive, Reg,' I said.

'I will, soon enough,' he replied.

CHAPTER 24

We set off for Wales on the Friday, after picking up all the groceries that we needed for the weekend. We arrived at about six in the evening. All was qu et.

'Seems that Dennis is well and truly laid to rest,' I said to Prue.

'Yes they've finally got him to rest ir peace.'

'I wonder where he's buried?' I said.

'In the small chapel graveyard in Penmachno,' replied Prue.

'How do you know that?' I queried.

'One of the locals told me the other week.'

'It would be nice if we could put some flowers on his grave,' I said.

'Yes he'd like that,' said Prue.

We had finished all the work in the bungalow so now all we had to do was relax, I got settled down to watch Corrie, whiskey in hand. We went to bed late that night. On the Saturday we got up at about nine, Reg and Marcia were due at eleven, so we had a gorgeous fry up. I felt as happy as a pig in shit! The grandfather clock struck Eleven and soon

Marcia was pulling up outside the front garden. We greeted our guests and soon we were tucking into ham sandwiches and a few beers.

After lunch we decided to go for a stroll to the chapel in Penmachno and I cut some roses from the front garden, on the way I told Reg and Marcia all about Dennis and the exorcism.

'Phew, I'd have shit my pants!' said Reg not too delicately.

'I did, mate,' I replied. 'But Prue took it all in her stride.'

'Women's intuition,' said Marcia.

We arrived at the small chapel and entered the graveyard, after a short search we came across Dennis's grave, it had a simple headstone with the inscription Mabel Giles 1940-1998, Dennis Giles 1940-2000 TOGETHER AT LAST. 'They are now,' whispered Prue.

I placed the flowers on the grave, something or someone whispered in my ear, 'Muchas gracias amigo!' I jumped back.

'What's up Dick,' said Reg, 'you look as if you've seen a ghost.'

'He's only saying thank you,' said Prue.

We took a leisurely stroll back to the bungalow, that evening we had a supper of steak and chips washed down with an excellent Merlot, after our meal the girls were in the kitchen washing up and Reg and I were in the lounge with a brandy each.

'Reg, I have been meaning to ask you, what exactly is string theory?' I queried.

Reg took a deep breath and said 'Ah, the great unknown, eh. Now where shall I begin:'

We live in a wonderfully complex universe, and we are curious about it by nature. Time and again we have wondered—why are we here? Where did we and the world come from? What is the world made of? It is our privilege to live in a time when enormous progress has been made towards finding some of the answers. String theory is our most recent attempt to answer the last (and part of the second) question.

So, what is the world made of? Ordinary matter is made of atoms, which are in turn made of just three basic components: electrons whirling around a nucleus composed of neutrons and protons. The electron is a truly fundamental particle (it is one of a family of particles known as leptons), but neutrons and protons are made of smaller particles known as quarks. Quarks are, as far as we know truly elementary.

Our current knowledge about the subatomic composition of the universe is summarized in what is known as the Standard Model of particle physics. It describes both the fundamental building blocks out of which the world is made, and the forces through which these blocks interact. There are twelve basic building blocks. Six of these are quarks—they go by the interesting names of up, down, charm, strange, bottom and top. (A proton, for instance, is made of two up quarks and one down quark.) The other six are leptons—these include the electron and its two heavier siblings, the muon and the tauon, as well as three neutrinos.

'Are you following me Dick?'

'So far Reg.'

'There are four fundamental forces in the universe: gravity, electromagnetism, and the weak and strong nuclear forces. Each of these is produced by fundamental particles that act as carriers of the force. The most familiar is the photon, a particle of light, which is the mediator of electromagnetic forces. (This means that, for instance, a magnet attracts a nail because both objects exchange photons.) The graviton is the particle associated with gravity. The strong force is carried by eight particles known as gluons. Finally, the weak force is transmitted by three particles, the W+, the W-, and the Z.

The behaviour of all these particles and forces is described with impeccable precision by the Standard Model, with one notable exception: gravity. For technical reasons, the gravitational force, the most familiar in our everyday lives, has proven very difficult to describe microscopically. This has been for many years one of the most important problems in theoretical physics—to formulate a quantum theory of gravity. In the last few decades, string theory has emerged as the most promising candidate for a microscopic theory of gravity. And it is infinitely more ambitious than that: it attempts to provide a complete unified, and consistent description of the fundamental structure of our universe.

(For this reason it is sometimes, quite arrogantly, called a 'theory of everything.')

'Are you still with me?"

"Yes, yes, carry on.'

'The essential idea behind string theory is this: all of the different 'fundamental' particles of The Standard Model are really just manifestations of one basic object, a string. How can that be? Well, we would ordinarily picture an electron, for instance, as a point with no internal structure. A point cannot do anything but move. But if string theory is correct, then under an extremely powerful 'microscope' we would realize that the electron is not really a point, but a tiny loop of string. A string can do something aside from moving—it can oscillate in different ways. If it oscillates a certain way, then for a distance, unable to tell it is really a string, we see an electron. But if it oscillates some other way, well, then we call it a photon, or a quark, or a . . . . you get the idea. So, if string theory is correct, the entire world is made of strings!

Perhaps the most remarkable thing about string theory is that such a simple idea works—it is possible to derive (an extension of) the Standard Model (which has been verified experimentally with incredible precision) from a theory of strings. But it should also be said that, to date, there is no direct experimental evidence that string theory itself is the correct description of nature. This is mostly due to the fact that string theory is still under development. We know bits and pieces of it, but we do not yet see the whole picture, and we are therefore unable to make definite predictions. In recent years many exciting developments have taken place,

159

radically improving our understanding of what the theory is.'
Ended Reg.

'So the jury is still out, then,' I replied.

'Exactly,' said Reg.

The girls finished the washing up and came into the lounge
so we cracked open another bottle of wine. Soon we were all
tiddly and laughing at nothing in particular. So the evening
passed and we decided to go to bed. As we got into bed
Prue said, 'Well, I think that went off quite well don't you?'

'Yeah,' I replied struggling to get my socks off.

We cuddled up together in bed. Just then I heard a moaning
sound coming from downstairs, I said to Prue, 'Oh no, don't
tell me that Dennis is back!'

'That's not Dennis, you prat,' said Prue, 'That's Marcia, her
and Reg are getting it on!'

'The randy devil,' I said.

CHAPTER 25

The following morning we were all down for breakfast and I couldn't help but give Reg a knowing smile. He looked away coyly. 'Oh, I forgot to tell you,' he said, 'I'm putting the house up for sale and Marcia's putting her flat up for sale too. We're moving to a detached we've got our eye on in Cheshire.'

'Ooh, that sounds lovely,' said Prue.

'You'll have to invite us round when you move in,' I said. I thought to myself, 'Fancy that. Reg living in the stockbroker belt.'

'Yes, we certainly will,' said Reg.

I must admit I felt a pang of remorse when I thought of his old house and the many cosy evenings I had spent there with him. After breakfast we all went out for a walk down the lane and stopped off at the pub. When we got inside the landlord said, 'Afternoon, one and all, and how did you get on with old ghostie then?'

I told the landlord of the past month's events, 'He was always a feisty bugger was Dennis,' he said, 'I had to call time on him at least half-a-dozen times before he'd shift his arse out of here. I'm glad he's at peace now.'

After a few drinks we strolled back to the bungalow and Marcia and Reg left at tea time.

We followed suit about an hour later, I had plenty of printing to do.

The years rolled on. It was now spring of 2011.

I was watching the news on the tele, an article came on about the Al-Qaeda leader Osama Bin Laden. It was about how he'd sanctioned the suicide raid on the twin towers in New York on 11 September 2001. He was at the top of America's 'most wanted' list. He had evaded the forces of the US and its allies for almost a decade, despite a £15m bounty on his head.

I had not dematerialised myself in years but I resolved to pay Bin Laden a visit.

I went into the garage and thought hard of Reg's theory and then of Pakistan, sure enough the familiar shroud of blue light engulfed me. I materialised in a small town called Abbottabad 100km north-east of Islamabad. I strolled up a dusty road until I came up to a compound about 1km from the Pakistan Military Academy. It was surrounded by 4m-6m walls and was eight times larger than other homes in the area. 'Fancy that,' I thought, 'the cheeky bugger's been living right under their noses all the time.' A truck was frozen in the act of going through the gate, so I slipped through no problem.

I let myself in through the main entrance to the house. There was a light on in one of the rooms at the front, inside was Bin Laden and his son, plus two couriers. I strolled in a circle round the terrorist, I thought, 'So this is the man who has sanctioned so many deaths, this frail old man. With that

I let him have it on the side of his head, his head shattered into tiny red fragments. I let his son and the two couriers have it, too. With that I walked out of the house and the gate and into the road outside. There I materialised so I could watch events unfold.

The truck drove through the main gate. To my astonishment six US Navy Seals ran in after it, and up and into the front door. There was a lot of shouting and the Seals came out carrying what appeared to be a body. I quickly transposed myself back into my garage.

I went indoors and sat down in my armchair after pouring myself a stiff whiskey, I was shaking a bit.

Prue came into the lounge and said, 'Are you alright, you look out of breath.'

'Oh, I was just doing some exercises in the garage,' I lied.

'Well they don't seem to be doing you any good,' she said.

After a couple more whiskies I felt calmer, soon it was time for bed.

The next morning I went down to the newsagents as usual for the newspaper. The headline screamed BIN LADEN SHOT BY US TROOPS. I got indoors to read the article it read:

Al-Qaeda leader Osama Bin Laden has been killed by US forces in Pakistan, President Barack Obama has said. Bin Laden was shot dead in the head at a compound near

Islamabad, in a ground operation based on US intelligence, the first lead for which emerged last August. Mr. Obama said US forces took possession of the body after 'a firefight.' He was top of the US' 'most wanted' list. DNA tests later confirmed that Bin Laden was dead, US officials said. Bin Laden was buried at sea after a Muslim funeral on board an aircraft carrier, Pentagon officials said.

'The crafty bastards,' I thought, 'they're making out that they killed him, I bet they were just going to arrest him not assassinate him.' Well, at least it took the heat off me.

I couldn't have been more wrong.

The news article went on:

World leaders welcomed the news of Bin Laden's death. Afghan President Hamid Karzai said Bin Laden had 'paid for his actions.' Pakistani Prime Minister Yusuf Raza Gilani said the killing was a 'great victory' but added that he 'didn't know the details' of the US operation. Former US President George W. Bush described the news as a 'momentous achievement.' 'The fight against terror goes on, but tonight America has sent an unmistakable message: No matter how long it takes, justice will be done,' Mr. Bush said in a statement.

But a spokesman for the Pakistani Taliban threatened revenge attacks against the 'American and Pakistani governments and their security forces.' In Gaza, which is governed by militant group Hamas, Prime Minister Ismail Haniya condemned the killing of 'a Muslim and Arabic Warrior.'

'What a cover up,' I thought.

Meanwhile, a week later, Manchester police had a visitor. It was the Director of Central Intelligence Leon Panetta from the Central Intelligence Agency in America. Present at the meeting was DI Harrison and M15 agent Rothwell. Panetta had some photographs to show. They were taken at the scene of Bin Laden's assassination. They showed the bloodbath in the room, decapitated bodies were all over the place. 'Look familiar?' said Panetta.

'Sure does,' said DI Harrison. 'It looks exactly the same as the scenes of crime over here some years ago.'

'And at Mugabe's assistants death,' piped up M15 agent Rothwell.

'I believe that we have a common perpetrator here,' said DCI Panetta.

'It certainly does,' agreed Harrison. 'But all our leads are stone cold, we have no idea where to turn to next.'

'Well I suggest that we all work as a team—we must share information and, who knows, we might just get a lead from somewhere,' said Panetta.

'Whoever or whatever is responsible is bound to slip up sooner or later,' said Rothwell.

"I cannot stress enough the secrecy we must observe about this case,' said Panetta. With that they all went about their daily business.

By now Reg had moved into his posh detached in Cheshire, it was a lovely four-bedroom pile that cost him and Marcia an arm and a leg. Prue and I had some lovely evenings there over the days. It was at one such evening that Marcia broke the news, 'I'm expecting,' she said, 'and it's a boy.'

"Ooh congratulations,' purred Prue.

'Well, you old so-of-a-gun, you,' I said.

'I know, it's wonderful isn't it?' said Reg.

'How many months are you,' inquired Prue.

"Oh, about three.'

With that Reg and I decided to wet the baby's head down at the local pub, we got a pint of bitter each and sat down in the corner.

'I've got more good news,' said Reg, 'We are going to visit The Large Hadron Collider in Geneva, Steven Hawking has made all the arrangements, we fly out there in a fortnight's time. We shall stay for a week, Hawking reckons it will prove my theory one way or the other.'

'That's great,' I replied. I felt honoured to be present on such a momentous occasion.

CHAPTER 26

Reg was now the head of the physics department at Walford University and was bestowing his knowledge on his students.

A week went by and I was reading an article in the newspaper about Gaddafhi, It read:

Muammar al-Gaddafhi is a Libyan politician and revolutionary, who has led the Libyan State since he overthrew King Idris in a 1969 bloodless coup and established the Libyan Arab republic. His 42 years in power make him one of the longest-serving rulers in history. Gaddafhi incorporated Arab socialist and Arab nationalist ideas into his political philosophy, which he published in The Green Book in 1975. In 1979 he relinquished the title of prime minister, and was thereafter called 'The Brother Leader' or 'The Guide' in Libya's Social Revolution.

Throughout the 1970s and 1980s, Libya under Gaddafhi was considered a pariah state by the West, which alleged oppression of internal dissidence, acts of state-sponsored terrorism, assassinations of expatriate opposition leaders, and crass nepotism exhibited in amassing a multi-billion-dollar fortune for himself and family. Gaddafhi was a firm supporter of OAPEC and led a Pan-African campaign for a United States of Africa. After the 1986 bombing of Libya and the 1993 imposition of United Nations sanctions, Gaddafhi established closer economic and security relations with the West, cooperated with investigations into previous Libyan acts of state-sponsored terrorism and paid compensation, and ended his nuclear weapons programme, resulting in the lifting of UN sanctions in 2003.

There was now civil war in Libya. Libyan rebels, no doubt encouraged by the success of their neighbours in Egypt, arose in revolt against Muammar al-Gaddafhi and his regime. Gaddafhi told the rebels to 'expect no mercy' and had killed thousands of his own countrymen. Even after the war is over Gaddafhi could still be in Tripoli.

The rebels obviously needed my help.

That morning, while Prue was out shopping, I entered the garage, I thought about the theory and of Tripoli in Libya.

I dematerialised outside Gaddafhi's palatial palace behind some shrubbery. There were soldiers everywhere, frozen in the various acts of going about their business. It didn't take me long to suss out where Gaddafhi was, I came to the main luxurious lounge, Gaddafhi was seated at the head of the table surrounded by his generals. I calmly walked up to where he sat. I struck him full in the face with my fist, as expected his head shattered into a myriad pieces. I materialised into the palace garden behind some bushes to watch events unfold.

Back in the three-dimensional world Gaddafhi and his generals were in hot debate about the war when, without warning Gaddafhi's head blew up showering his henchmen in blood and bits of brain. The generals screamed like a crowd of girls at a hen party. One yelled, 'It's the Americans secret weapon!' 'Allah save us,' another one cried. The place was in turmoil with soldiers and high-ranking officials running about like headless chickens. The rebels stormed the palace and paraded Gaddafhi's body through the streets.

I dematerialised back to my garage.

That evening I was watching television when a newsflash came on:

Today at 11 a.m. Libyan leader Muammar al-Gaddafhi was found murdered in his boardroom by his staff. He had suffered massive trauma to the head The perpetrator has not been found, the rebels dragged Gaddafhi's body through the streets claiming to have shot him in the head.

'Result!' I thought to myself.

The next morning the newspapers read: GADDAFHI REGIME TUMBLES.

The article accompanying it read:

Gaddafhi's generals this morning stood down from Government in Tripoli and announced that 'full and fair' elections would take place as to who will rule Libya.

'Well that's saved a lot of lives on both sides,' I thought to myself.

I was just about to go into the garage to do some printing when the phone rang. It was reg.

'You've been at it again haven't you?' he said.

'I might have.'

'Just watch your step Dick,' he warned. 'The police will be getting help from a higher authority I shouldn't wonder.'

'What do you mean by that?' I queried.

'You know, some sort of intelligence agency like M15.'

'OK, I'll watch my back,' I said.

With that Reg rang off.

CHAPTER 27

The next day Prue and I went down to Wales to visit the bungalow, it was looking good in the garden with the many rose bushes in full bloom, I pushed the previous days' events to the back of my mind and tried to enjoy the day. I decided to paint the outside window frames, doors and guttering. The sun was beating down so we decided to have lunch of ham sandwiches and beer in the garden. After three days graft I finished the painting, I went indoors, showered and sat down in the armchair with—you ve guessed it—a large whiskey. I was thinking of the Large Hadron Collider and our visit there the next week, 'What does it actually do?' I thought. 'I'll have to get Reg to brief me before we get there.' All I know is that it accelerates particles and makes them smash together.

We had a couple more idyllic days at the bungalow and then we had to go home because I wanted to get the printing down before going to Geneva.

That was, when we were on our way home, Prue said, 'Dick, I've been thinking, why don't we live at the bungalow permanently? The house is too big for us now that the girls have left, so we should sell it and live off the proceeds.'

'What about the printing business,' I replied.

"Oh, that. You could sell that too, I reckon you could get about ten grand for it. Besides you will be 60 next birthday.'

Surprised by what Prue said I replied, 'I suppose we could, but just give me time to get my head round it, will you?'

I was definitely warming to her idea.

At Manchester Police Headquarters M15 agent Rothwell was paying DI Harrison a visit, DCI Panetta was on video link. 'Well he's been at it again,' opened Panetta.

'And, as usual, we have no leads, not even any DNA,' said Rothwell.

'I'm beginning to think it's a Government secret weapon,' said DI Harrison.

'I can assure you, if it were I would know about it,' retorted Panetta.

'Same goes for me,' said agent Rothwell.

'I still think it's a highly trained assassin,' said Panetta.

'Yeah, me too,' said Rothwell.

'Well, all we can do is what we have always done, keep on our toes and share any information that may turn up,' finished Panetta. 'I'll be in touch.' With that, the screen went blank.

The police and the Central Intelligence Agency were just as far from apprehending anybody as they'd always been.

The crime figures were going up again. 'I shall have to pay someone a visit,' I thought. 'We can't have that can we?'

CHAPTER 28

Reg went to the asylum to visit his cousin Regina. 'Where have you been this past couple of months?' she chided.

'Me, oh, I've been extremely busy, what with the University and everything,' said Reg.

'Have you brought me my jammy doughnuts?' enquired Regina.

'Certainly have, fresh today.'

Regina tucked into the doughnuts with relish.

'I saw Winston Churchill today, and Joseph Stalin, they were talking about the war.'

'Oh, did you now,' humoured Reg, 'How's the war going then?'

'We're winning,' came the reply. 'I'm going to assassinate Hitler next week, just like that assassin in the papers!'

Just then the nurse came round with Regina's medication. 'How's she doing lately?' Reg asked of the nurse.

'She's fine, she still thinks it's 1943, but she's eating and sleeping OK.' From her tray the nurse selected two tablets, 'come on now Regina time for your medicine.'

Regina obediently opened her mouth and the nurse popped them in.

As soon as the nurse turned her back Regina spat them out, 'No happy pills for me, no sir,' she said.

'You naughty girl,' said Reg, 'Those are to keep you calm.'

'Dammit, I'm as calm as can be. I don't need no pills,' retorted Regina.

'Dick and I are off to Geneva next week,' said Reg.

'I suppose you are going over there to talk a load of rubbish with your like-minded mates are you?' said an unimpressed Regina.

'We're going to visit a fabulous machine called the Large Hadron Collider.'

'The Large Hadron what?' retorted Regina, 'sounds a load of old codswallop to me.'

'She's always like this,' Reg thought, 'so sarcastic all the time.'

After about half-an-hour's chat Reg decided to leave.

'Go on then, leave me in this dump, It's driving me crazy in here,' said Regina to no one in particular.

'Now you know you're in here for your own good Regina,' replied Reg. 'They look after you here don't they?'

'I'm sick of nurses shoving pills in my mouth and I'm sick of the grub here, too it tastes like crap,' said Regina.

She always behaved like this when her visitors were leaving. Just before he left Reg popped into the nurse's office and told them what Regina was doing with her medication.

'Ahh, no wonder her medication isn't working, right, we'll keep an eye on her in future, I can assure you Mr. Stein that she will be taking her pills from now on,' said one of the staff.

'Poor Regina,' thought Reg. 'I hate leaving her there, but what can I do, she's definitely a basket case.'

CHAPTER 29

Saturday soon came around and we prepared for our trip to Geneva. The taxi came for me and then picked up Reg at his house. And then on to the airport, it had been years since I had flown and I was quite looking forward to it.

The plane was dead on time and soon the stewardess was serving drinks, I ordered two whiskies and tonics for Reg and I. 'Funny how it always seemed to taste nicer on the plane,' I thought. After a short flight we touched down at the French airport where we got a taxi that had been laid on by Stephen Hawking, to take us on to our hotel in Geneva.

When we got to the hotel we booked in and went up to our room which was furnished with twin beds a mini bar and a satellite TV. 'Oh, goody,' I thought 'I shall be able to keep up with Corrie, this is great.'

We wandered downstairs and into the lounge bar which was full of physicists and professors, all wanting to meet Reg, we spotted Stephen Hawking in the corner of the room deep in conversation, via his computer, with a very learned-looking man who we late found out to be the Director of the Institute. We went over to them and we were introduced to Doctor Chapman.

'We will be accelerating lead nuclei and smashing them together at just below the speed of light. This will give us conditions the same as at the creation of the universe, or the big bang as it is popularly called. Antimatter will be created and also other strange particles like quarks, but, and this is the most important aspect of what we are doing, if anti photons are created, this will be proof that your theory of a relative absolute rest of the universe exists,' said Dr. Chapman.

Soon it was time for dinner, and after an excellent meal washed down with a delightful Burgundy. We retired with brandy in hand, to the lounge where we were joined by two young physicists and Dr. Chapman. There was much talk of the Large Hadron Collider and the results it had produced over the years it had been in operation. It was to run Reg's experiment next Wednesday. Apparently there was a particle called the Higgs Boson which was proving elusive to track down.

I said to the group and no one in particular, 'Could you please explain what the LHC does in layman's terms please.'

Doctor Chapman said, 'It would give me great pleasure my dear sir. The Large Hadron Collider (LHC) is a gigantic scientific instrument near Geneva, where it spans the border between Switzerland and France about 100m underground. It is a particle accelerator. It is used by physicists to study the smallest known particles—the fundamental building blocks of all things. It will revolutionise our understanding, from the miniscule world deep within atoms to the vastness of the universe.

Two beams of sub-atomic particles called 'hadrons'—either protons or lead ions—will travel in opposite directions inside the circular accelerator, gaining energy with every lap. Physicists will use the LHC to recreate the conditions just

177

after the Big Bang, by colliding the two beams head on at very high energy. Teams of physicists from around the world will analyse the particles created in the collisions using special detectors in a number of experiments dedicated to the LHC, your experiment being one of them.

There are many theories as to what will result from these collisions, but what's for sure is that a brave new world of physics will emerge from the new accelerator, as knowledge in particle physics goes on to describe the workings of the universe. For decades, the Standard Model of particle physics has served physicists well as a means of understanding the fundamental laws of Nature, but it does not tell the whole story. Only experimental data using the higher energies reached by the LHC can push knowledge forward, challenging those who dare to dream beyond the paradigm.

CERN is an international laboratory for particle physicists, providing some of the most technologically advanced facilities for their research into the basic building blocks of the universe. Specialist facilities that would otherwise be difficult or impossible for individual nations to build include particle accelerators such as the Large Hadron Collider, and facilities for the production of exotic forms of matter, including antimatter.

CERN has established a reputation at the forefront of research, proven through its experiments, past and present. The laboratory is a vibrant meeting place for discussion and debate; around half of the world's particle physicists come here for their research. This is reflected in the experiments, which are usually run by international collaborations, bringing together teams of physicists from different institutes towards a common goal.

'Imagination is more important than knowledge.' These were the words of the famous physicist Albert Einstein, who went on to say that 'Knowledge is limited. Imagination encircles the world.'

Dr. Chapman went on:

If you venture into the sub atomic world in an attempt to unveil its inner workings, possession of all the knowledge in the world is not enough. Instead, invite your imagination to serve as a guide, because many rules as we know them no longer apply. Just like the story of Alice in Wonderland, this new world may look familiar but is not fully comprehensible. Scales shift and matter transforms. Transitory twins appear and extra dimensions hide. Just like your fifth dimension.

Nature has the ability to throw us the biggest surprises, so expect dramatic twists and unexpected turns; many before you have dreamed up mind-blowing theories and crazy concepts. Some of these have prevailed against the tests of time and armies of knowledgeable critics—thus far.

'Someone, sometime, somewhere, may succeed in completing these unfinished mysteries, or even rewrite the chapters entirely. The book is by no means finished,' ended Dr. Chapman.

'You can say that again,' I thought, the physicists were nowhere near discovering the actual cause and effect of the theory.

'So will the accelerated particles enter the fifth dimension,' asked Reg.

I could see that Reg was in his element, talking about the Theory to the physicists.

'Not the accelerated particles but the particles that are created in the collision, the quarks and hopefully, the Higgs Boson,' said Dr. Chapman, 'We expect to see a blue shift in the accelerator. We shall run your experiment on Wednesday at 10 a.m. exactly.'

'I'm going to phone Prue and tell her we arrived safely,' I said to Reg.

'Good idea, I am going to call Marcia,' he replied. 'I want to see if she's OK what with the baby and everything.'

Reg reluctantly tore himself away from the group of physicists to make the call. Both the girls were alright, so we rejoined our companions in the lounge, I went to the bar and ordered two Jack Daniel whiskies which were on Stephen Hawkins' tab. The conversation turned towards Quantum mechanics, and that was where the physicists lost me. Reg had picked up all this knowledge in the later stages of his life, he had come from a bumkin to a respected top physicist in the matter of a few years.

Soon it was time for bed, we had to be up early because we were going on a guided tour of the LHC on the Sunday morning. We awoke to the sound of my clock-radio playing 'Judas' by Lady GaGa. We had a Continental breakfast and soon it was time for our tour. First we visited the control room which was staffed by the brains of the outfit Brian Charnock and Alan Brooks. They gave an impressive lecture on what was showing on their computer screens which showed the ionised trails of the particles as they were created. Then Dr. Chapman ushered us out and into the curved corridor which housed the LHC. We boarded a buggy which transported us along the corridor, with Dr. Chapman giving a running commentary on the way. Soon we came to the part of the LHC where it all happens: the 'target' area where the lead nuclei collide.

'It is here where we shall witness the act of Creation,' said Dr. Chapman somberly.

'What is this particle, the Higgs Boson,' I asked.

'Well, look at it this way,' said Dr. Chapman. 'When you get on the scale in the morning, you may be hoping that it registers a smaller number than the day before—you may be hoping that you've lost weight. It's the quantity of mass in you, plus the force of gravity, that determines your weight. But what determines your mass?

That's one of the most-asked, most-hotly pursued questions in physics today. Many of the experiments circulating in the world's particle accelerators are looking into the mechanism that gives rise to mass. Scientists at CERN, as well as at Fermilab in Illinois, are hoping to find what they call the 'Higgs boson.' Higgs, they believe, is a particle, or set of particles, that might give others mass.

The idea of one particle giving another mass is a bit counter-intuitive . . . isn't mass an inherent characteristic of matter? If no, how can one entity impart mass on all others by simply floating by and interacting with them?'

Dr. Chapman went on: 'An oft-cited analogy describes it well: Imagine you're at a Hollywood party. The crowd is rather thick, and evenly distributed around the room, chatting. When the big star arrives, the people nearest the door gather around her. As she moves through the party, she attracts the people closest to her, and those that she moves away from return to their conversations. By gathering a fawning cluster of people around her, she's gained momentum, an indication of mass. She's harder to slow down than she would be without the crowd. Once she's stopped, it's harder to get her going again.

The clustering effect is the Higgs mechanism, postulated by British physicist Peter Higgs in the 1960s. The theory hypothesizes that a sort of lattice, referred to as the Higgs field, fills the universe. This is something like an electromagnetic field, in that it affects the particles that move through it, but it is also related to the physics of solid materials. Scientists know that when an electron passes through a positively-charged crystal lattice of atoms (a solid), the electron's mass can increase as much as 40 times. The same might be true in the Higgs field: a particle moving through it creates a little bit of distortion—like the crowd around the star at the party—and that lends mass to the particle.

The question of mass has been an especially puzzling one, and has left the Higgs boson as the single missing piece of the Standard Model yet to be spotted.

The Standard Model describes three of Nature's four forces: electromagnetism and the strong and weak nuclear forces. Electromagnetism has been fairly well understood for many decades. Recently, physicists have learned much more about the strong force, which binds the elements of atomic nuclei together, and the weak force, which governs radioactivity and hydrogen fusion (which generates the sun's energy).

Electromagnetism describes how particles interact with photons, tiny packets of electromagnetic radiation. In a similar way, the weak force describes how two other entities, the W and Z particles, interact with electrons, quarks, neutrinos and others. There is one very important difference between these two interactions: photons have no mass, while the masses of W and Z are huge, in fact, they are some of the most massive known.

The first inclination is to assume that W and Z simply exist and interact with other elemental particles. But for mathematical reasons, the giant masses of W and Z raise inconsistencies in the Standard Model. To address this, physicists postulate that there must be at least one other particle—the Higgs boson.

The simplest theories predict only one boson, but others say there might be several. In fact, the search for the Higgs particle or particles is some of the most exciting research happening, because it could lead to completely new discoveries in particle physics. Some theorists say it could bring to light entirely new types of strong interactions, and others believe research will reveal a new fundamental physical symmetry called 'supersymmetry.'

First, though, scientists want to determine whether the Higgs boson exists. The search has been on for over ten years, both at CERN's Large Electron Positron Collider (LEP) in Geneva and at Fermilab Illinois. To look for the particle, researchers must smash other particles together at very high speeds. If the energy from that collision is high enough, it is converted into smaller bits of matter—particles—one of which could be a Higgs boson. The Higgs will only last for a small fraction of a second, and then decay into other particles. So in order to tell whether the Higgs appeared in the collision, researchers look for evidence of what it would have decayed into. And this is where your theory comes in, when the Higgs boson decays it should emit anti-photons.

In August 2000, physicists working at CERN's LEP saw traces of particles that might fit the right pattern, but the evidence is still inconclusive. LEP was closed down in the beginning of November, 2000, but the search continues at Fermilab in Illinois, and will pick up again at CERN when the LHC (Large Hadron Collider) begins the experiment in 2011.'

'I trust that answers your question, my friend?' concluded Dr. Chapman.

'That was very informative,' I replied.

And so the tour ended, 'what a fascinating morning,' I thought.

We all went down to the dining room for lunch, Reg was in deep conversation with the two control room physicists.

We sat down to a meal of spaghetti Bolognese washed down with a nice Chianti followed, of course, with a five-star brandy. 'I could get used to this,' I thought. The afternoon was spent sight-seeing in Geneva and a stop at a little pub for a few lagers.

CHAPTER 30

Monday came and we had a chance to talk to the engineers that had actually installed the LHC. They told us that the machine was 27km in diameter and that the speed of the particles would eventually travel were 11000 revolutions a second! At 99% the speed of light.

Soon it was Wednesday morning, 9 a.m. We left the hotel and arrived at the LHC for 9:30 a.m., there, was Doctor Chapman who showed us into the control room. The room was packed with physicists and engineers.

'First we have to strip the atoms of lead down to their bare nuclei, this ionises the particles then we accelerate them up to the speed of 99% the speed of light. There are three main detectors, the Atlas, the LHCb—which searches for anti-matter and the CMS which will detect the 'god particle' or the Higgs boson,' said Dr. Chapman.

The atmosphere in the room was electric as the seconds ticked away towards 10 a.m.

"OK let us proceed gentlemen,' said Dr. Chapman. All that could be heard was a faint hum coming from the machine and the occasional cough.

'20% speed of light' said Brian the control room technician. Then '40% speed of light.' About 10 minutes went by. '80% speed of light' said the technician. Then '90% the speed of light' and five minutes later, 99% speed of light, ready to collide particles.

'OK operate the Atlas detector,' said Dr. Chapman. 'Any readings?'

'Yes but I'm not sure yet,' said the technician, 'There's plenty of data coming in but I'll have to ana yse it before we can be certain of what we're detecting.'

'Operate LHCb,' said an excited Dr. Chapman.

'LHCb in operating mode,' said the technician.

'Anything?' said Chapman.

'Massive amounts of data coming in,' said the technician. Then, 'Yes here we go—We have photons anti-quarks and, Holy Moly, anti-photons!'

The room erupted into cheers from the assembled personnel and scientists were shaking Reg by the hand and back-slapping him.

'OK, now for the main event, operate the CMS detector,' said Dr. Chapman.

'CMS in operation,' said Brian. 'Detection of massive particles, decaying almost instantaneously. We can't tell if it's the Higgs boson yet.'

'It must be,' said Reg to me, 'if they've detected anti-photons the particle must exist.'

All too soon the experiment was over, the scientists were all talking at once and crowding round the monitors, trying to analyse the data on the screens. Printers chattered furiously churning out streams of figures and data. Reg sought out Dr. Chapman who was engrossed in a sheet of information that had been printed out.

'Well Dr. Chapman does the Higgs boson Exist?' said Reg.

'Um, we can't be sure yet,' he replied. 'I shall have to analyse this data first before we issue a Press release.'

Reg walked over to where I was standing and whispered in my ear, 'They're hiding something, I know it!'

The week went by, Filled with discussion about the Higgs boson and anti-photons. And soon it was time for home. There was still no Press release from Dr. Chapman.

'I can't understand it,' said Reg on the plane. 'The Higgs boson must exist if there were anti-photons detected. The two go together like hand and glove.'

'Perhaps they have to analyse the vast amounts of data that was churned out yet,' I said.

"Hmm, maybe you're right,' said Reg resignedly, 'It's early days yet.

CHAPTER 31

The flight arrived at Manchester Airport and we got our taxis for home. It was eight pm.

I went indoors and Prue greeted me, 'Like a drink, love,' she said, planting a big kiss on my cheek.

'Oooh, ta,' I replied.

Prue fixed me up a whiskey and tonic, 'Well, did you enjoy your week away,' she said.

'It was great,' I replied, 'but I'm glad to be back home.'

'Oh, by the way, I saved you yesterday's Telegraph there's an article in it I'm sure you will be interested in.'

I opened the paper and there it was, the headline read: LARGE HADRON COLLIDER RUMOURED TO HAVE FOUND GOD PARTICLE. I sat bolt upright in my chair. The article, by Richard Gray the science Correspondent read:

Scientists at the Large Hadron Collider are rumoured to have found the elusive so-called 'God Particle.'

A leaked internal memo contains unconfirmed reports that one of the detectors at the Large Hadron Collider at CERN, near Geneva, had picked up signals that could be the long sought after particle, called the Higgs boson.

One of the main scientific goals of the huge £6 billion atom smasher was to prove the existence of the Higgs boson, a theoretical particle believed to give everything in the Universe mass.

The particle is a key part of the Standard Model used in physics to describe how particles and atoms are made up.

Rumours that scientists working on the LHC had found evidence of the Higgs boson began to circulate after a supposed internal memo was posted on the internet.

But physicists were quick to urge caution over the claims as many candidates for the particle that appear in collision experiments at the LHC are subsequently dismissed on further examination.

Officials at CERN said the result had not yet been properly verified and could turn out to be a false alarm.

The memo revealed that one of the particle detectors at the LHC had caught a particle that could be a Higgs boson decaying into two high-energy particles known as photons and anti-photons.

The memo, written by four scientists working on the LHC's ATLAS experiment, warned the rate at which this happened was thirty times larger than would have been expected.

But it added: 'The present result is the first definitive observation of physics beyond the Standard Model.

Exciting new physics, including new particles, may be expected to be found in the very near future.'

Some scientists initially said they believed the memo could be a hoax, but it was confirmed as genuine by officials at CERN.

Dr. Chapman, official spokesman for CERN, said that while the results note was genuine, it was one of thousands constantly being produced by scientists and that it was still in the very early stages of assessment.

He said 'It is far too early to say if there is anything to it or not, there are 3000 scientists working on ATLAS and they divide the analysis work up between them.

This is an internal communication that highlights something interesting, but it has to go through several stages of assessment by the team before it will be released as an official result by the collaborative team.

The majority of these things turn out to be nothing at all. It is very speculative at this stage, but there is a great deal of excitement and anticipation that something will be found which is probably why this has found its way onto the internet.'

Despite the official caution, there was intense speculation on internet blogs and scientific websites that the results described in the memo signaled the first discovery of the Higgs boson.

The rumours come as officials in CERN revealed they had set a new world record by producing the most intense beams of particles ever achieved.

191

The memo first appeared on the blog of physicist Peter Woit, from Columbia University. He wrote 'It's the sort of thing you would expect to see if there were a Higgs at that mass, but the number of events seen is about 30 times more than the standard Model would predict. 'Professor Brian Cox, a particle physicist at Manchester University and presenter of the BBCs Wonders of the Universe, urged caution over the results.

Writing on the social networking site Twitter, he said, 'The Higgs rumours are from an internal, unchecked ATLAS document. Very bad science to leak it. Many mistakes are made in un-reviewed papers.'

Dr. Chapman stated that 'because of the creation of anti-photons however, Reginal Stein's theory has proved to be correct, and the fifth dimension does exist.

I got on the phone to Reg right away and read the article to him.

'I'm telling you Dick,' he said, 'They're hiding something, I wish I was a fly on the wall at CERN. Why would they want to hide the fact that they've discovered the Higgs boson, after all, there are 3000 scientists there, it's bound to leak out.'

'How's Marcia?' I enquired, changing the subject.

'Oh, she's fine, I just felt the baby kick, it was wonderful,' replied Reg, 'Anyway, I'll get on to Stephen Hawking and see what he has to say about all of this.'

CHAPTER 32

It was now June 2011 and Marcia had given birth to a bouncing baby boy of 8 lb. The couple were blissfully happy and I was to be the proud godfather. Prue and I were spending more and more time down at the bungalow and we decided to put the house and printing business up for sale. We were hoping to get £140,000 for the house and 10 grand for the print business.

Reg and Stephen Hawking agreed with one another that the Higgs boson had been detected in the LHC, but there was still no official Press release by Dr. Chapman.

Two days went by and Reg received an E-mail from Dr. Chapman that he was coming to the UK to present a paper to the journal 'Nature' and that he would visit Reg at Walford University.

'Dr. Chapman is visiting on Wednesday and I would like it if you could be present at the meeting at the University,' said Reg to me on the phone.

'I would be delighted,' I replied, 'It'll be interesting to hear what he has to say at the least.'

Wednesday came and found Reg and I waiting expectantly for Dr. Chapman to put in an appearance in one of the lecture rooms. There was a knock on the door and Dr. Chapman entered.

'Well, gentlemen I won't beat about the bush as they say, all the available data suggests the existence of the Higgs boson.'

'What do you mean 'Suggests?' queried Reg, 'It either exists or it doesn't.'

'Very well, it does exist, definitely,' said Dr. Chapman.

'Why are you so reticent about it, then, what's all the secrecy for.

Dr. Chapman sighed, 'My dear chap the reason we have held back is because of the Military.'

'The Military? I don't understand,' said Reg.

'Just think of it, the Higgs boson decays in fractions of a second giving rise to matter and antimatter which in turn causes a nuclear reaction the like we have never seen before.'

'You mean . . . .'

'Yes my dear sir, a nuclear bomb so powerful that it would make conventional nuclear weapons seem like a child's firework,' exclaimed Dr. Chapman, It would be the destroyer of Worlds.'

There was a stunned silence, I could see Reg's mind analysing this shocking statement.

'I, I don't know what to say,' said a stunned Reg.

'I shall be publishing the paper on the discovery of the Higgs Boson in 'Nature,' I have to as there are hundreds of physicists that know about it. If I don't publish then any one of them will.'

With that, Dr. Chapman said his goodbyes and left.

'No wonder they held back,' said Reg. 'You know full well what happens when matter interacts with matter in the fifth dimension, there is a super reaction. The consequences are unbelievable.'

'How long would it take to develop a weapon such as this, then,' I asked.

'A matter of years—no wonder there is always ready money to invest in these particle accelerators, the Military and Governments already have their snout in the trough,' said Reg.

I drove home in my Fiesta with the radio off, mulling over what had been said at Walford University. 'It's going to be a dangerous world for Reg to bring his son up in,' I thought.

I got home and Prue was waiting for me with my usual tipple, 'How did the meeting go?' she asked.

'Oh, Dr. Chapman's going to publish at last, confirming the existence of the Higgs boson.'

'That's good news isn't it?' said Prue.

'Yeah, I suppose it is.'

Rick Groves

'Then why do you look as if you've seen your backside?' she retorted.

'Oh, I'm just tired that's all. I'll be alright when I've had a few of these.'

I drowned my sorrows that night, I can tell you.

CHAPTER 33

In the morning the papers were all telling the same story, GOD PARTICLE FOUND said one, CAN IT BE ARMAGEDDON blared another. So Dr. Chapman had given the Press release at last. It was official, the Higgs boson existed and the consequences for mankind lay in the not too distant future.

The phone rang. It was Reg, 'Can you come over tonight Dick, I want to see you about something, remember a few years ago when we agreed to dematerialise together? Well, I want to have a go tonight, Marcia's out for the evening at her mother's, so we won't be disturbed.

'Yes OK,' I replied, 'where are we going?'

'Wait till you get here, I'll tell you then, It'll be mind blowing I can assure you.'

That afternoon there was a phone call from a young man in Liverpool, he seemed very interested in the printing business, so I arranged to meet him the next day in the garage. That evening I got in the car and journeyed to Reg's.

When I got there Reg offered me a Jack Daniels 'Just a small one, I'm driving,' I said to Reg.

We went into the lounge and sat down, sipping the whiskey I regretted not getting a taxi.

'Right, Reg where are we off to, then?' I enquired.

'Somewhere fabulous,' he replied. 'We are going to the birth of the Universe. To be exact, 2 minutes before the Big Bang actually.'

'2 minutes before Creation,' I exclaimed. 'How can we go to something that existed before we were created?' I asked.

'Remember, we will be materialising in the fifth dimension, observing a four dimensional happening. Time has no meaning, I'm telling you, it will work.'

'Well, I hope so for both our sakes,' I said in alarm.

'I assure you nothing can go wrong, just believe in the theory,' said Reg.

We both stood up and went to the centre of the lounge where we thought hard about the theory and then the beginning of time and space itself. The blue shift shrouded us both.

We materialised into blackness, 2 minutes before the creation of the universe, an all pervading inky, heavy blackness. We couldn't see each other as light did not exist yet. 'Can you hear me?' said Reg.

'Yes, I can,' I replied.

'Look there,' said reg, 'what's that?'

It was a human face, floating in the blackness! It's eyes were wide open, the mouth was also wide open as if screaming.

We both materialised to 1 minute before creation, the face was still there, the mouth agape, with a white glow coming from inside it. We then materialised to a billionth of a second after Creation. A plasma of some sort was spewing out of the face's mouth creating matter and anti-matter, light photons and time now existed. Then a minute after Creation, the face now couldn't be seen, it had disappeared in a maelstrom of hydrogen plasma. Reg and I were engulfed in the explosion that was the birth of the Universe, we quickly materialised back into Reg's lounge.

'That was incredible,' I gasped.

'Fantastic,' said Reg. 'The birth of the Universe itself, I can't believe it. We witnessed Creation.'

'But what was the face all about?'

'The Universe was created by human intellect, some 13.7 billion years ago, that can be the only answer!' said Reg.

'So is that what we are evolving towards now?'

'Without a doubt,' said Reg, 'Our evolution is steering us towards becoming a race of super-intellectual beings. The second generation human beings, is what we are.'

'It's just like first and second generation stars,' I said, 'The first generation gave birth to the second generation enriching them with the heavy elements that in turn made up our human bodies—we are definitely the children of the stars.'

'That's correct, Dick, the human intellect that we have witnessed must exist in a parallel universe that lies alongside ours like the two sides of a piece of paper.'

'It's such a shame that we can't let the rest of the scientific community know about what we have discovered,' I said.

'Well I have been keeping a diary ever since I read that first article about the Theory of Relativity,' said Reg, 'I intend leaving it to posterity.'

'Now that the Higgs boson has been proven to exist and the possible invention of a super-nuclear weapon there might not be any posterity to leave it to,' I said.

'True,' said Reg, 'that's for the future though.'

'I think that the scientific community should petition the nuclear powers not to create a super-nuclear weapon and make them aware of the disastrous situation for mankind,' I said.

"I agree,' said Reg, 'I'll put the wheels in motion first thing tomorrow.'

With that I bade Reg goodnight and journeyed home, deep in thought.

CHAPTER 34

The next day dawned and at the afternoon the young lad called round to look at the printing equipment.

'I have all the customers printing plates here, so as you can see it's quite a going concern,' I said to the lad.

'I'm very interested but I can't afford ten grand,' he said, 'How about eight?'

'Call it nine grand and you've got a deal.'

'OK,' he replied. He then wrote a cheque for the full amount, 'I'll call round tomorrow to pick it all up.

'You'll have to get a tail lift van,' I said.

'That's all right I'll go to the van hire rental company,' he replied.

The next day he came round and we loaded all the equipment on to the van, along with all the negatives and printing plates and loads of different inks. We shook hands and he left. The garage was empty and silent. I felt a twinge of regret and wondered if I'd done the right thing. Never mind, nine grant was not to be sniffed at especially as I'd only paid a quid for it! Time to persue my role of becoming an old age pensioner.

In the meantime the police and the intelligence agencies were no nearer to solving the cases of the exploding heads cases. The trail had gone 'stone cold' as DI Harrison said. Crime figures were creeping up again. It was time for another 'visit' to some retard or other.

That night I entered the garage and dematerialised to the bottom of the road where I lived. I took a casual stroll up to the park and went through the gate. I strolled up the pathway leading into the park's centre, bingo! Four youths were caught in the act of torching a car they had stolen. I casually walked up to one of them and smacked him in the head which exploded into thousands of fragments. I then circled two more of them, 'Now then, who's going to be the lucky one then?' I thought. I hit another of the youths and then a third, I left the fourth to tell the tale of what happened to his mates.

I went behind some bushes and materialised to observe what was happening. The remaining youth was on his knees, sobbing like a baby, a discarded petrol can lay by his side. The car was well alight. He was surrounded by what remained of his pals his T-shirt was covered in blood. By now several people were gathering round. 'Jesus, what a blood bath,' said one. 'Looks like that vigilante has struck again,' said another. I walked up to the growing crowd to see the result of my handiwork.

'I, I dunno what happened,' cried the youth, 'we weren't doing nuffink and their heads just blew up!'

'Lying little toe rag,' I thought.

Someone phoned the police, who arrived minutes later. 'Better contact DI Harrison,' said one officer. One of the officers contacted DI Harrison at police headquarters.

'Shit not again,' he exclaimed, 'I'll be there as soon as I can.'

It took ten minutes and DI Harrison was at the scene of the crime, 'Christ,' he said it's the same thing, all of them with severe trauma to the head.' Turning towards the remaining youth he said, 'Did you see anything at all? Anything unusual?'

'No, officer, nothing except for the . . . .'

'For what?' said DI Harrison. 'Come on cough it up lad.'

'I saw a strange blue light over by the bushes, just there,' he pointed towards the bushes where I had materialised.

'Are you sure it wasn't just one of the flashing blue lights on our patrol car that you saw?' queried DI Harrison.

'No mate, it was well before you got here,' said the youth.

'Hmm, interesting,' said DI Harrison, Turning to one of the policemen he said, 'Go over to those bushes and see what you can find.'

'Yes boss,' said one of the officers. About five minutes later the policeman shouted, 'I've got something boss!'

Harrison walked brusquely over to the bushes, 'What have you got?'

'Footprints, boss, fresh as a daisy in the mud.'

'Yes somebody was hiding behind these bushes just a few minutes ago,' said DI Harrison.

I took this as a cue to leave the scene, and I strolled casually back home where I washed the mud off my shoes using the garden tap. Just to be absolutely certain I put the shoes in the bin, which was due for collection the next day.

DI Harrison formally arrested the remaining youth for taking without consent. Great!

Two days later, DI Harrison had a meeting with M15 Agent Rothwell, as usual DCI Panettte was on video link. 'So what have you got?' opened Panetta.

'Well, one of the remaining youths saw what he called, a strange blue light coming from behind some bushes, and when we inspected the scene we found the fresh footprints of someone who had been hiding there, we have taken plaster casts of the footprints,' said Harrison.

'That's better than the usual nothing,' said "Agent Rothwell.

'We are conducting house to house searches in the local area to see if we can match the shoes to the casts,' said Harrison, 'and, oh yes, they were Clarks shoes.'

'Let me know if anything new turns up,' said Panetta.

'I certainly will,' said Harrison, and with that the men ended their meeting.

The papers were having a field day with the vigilante angle featuring prominently in their articles, one even coined the phrase 'SUPER VIGILANTE STRIKES AGAIN.'

Two weeks went by and the police's trail had gone stone cold, in fact they were freezing. Crime figures plummeted to an all time low. In the letters pages of the newspapers members of the public sang their praises of the vigilante.

I dematerialised several times during the fortnight looking for retards on the streets but everything was quiet.

We had put the house up for sale in the local estate agents, a week later, after a few timewasters, a young couple put a deposit down. Four weeks later the house was sold and we were ready to move out, Prue and I felt a few pangs of sorrow, after all it was where we had brought the girls up and had a special place in our hearts.

We moved ourselves in a tail-lift van with Reg giving me a hand, we didn't need much furniture as we had furnished most of the bungalow previously. As I drove Reg was nattering away about the Large Hadron Collider: 'Guess what the LHC has created now Dick?'

'I dunno, what?'

'Dark matter,' Reg replied.

'Oh yes and what exactly is dark matter?' I queried.

'Remarkably, it turns out there is five times more material in clusters of galaxies than we would expect from the galaxies and hot gas we can see. Most of the stuff in clusters of galaxies is invisible and, since these are the largest structures in the Universe held together by gravity, scientists then conclude that most of the matter in the entire Universe is invisible. This invisible stuff is called 'dark matter,' a term initially coined by Fritz Zwicky who discovered evidence for missing mass in galaxies in the 1930s. There is currently much ongoing research by scientists to discover exactly what this dark matter is, how much there is, and what effect it may have on the future of the Universe as a whole,' said Reg.

'So do we know how much of this dark matter there is in the Universe,' I asked.

'Estimates are that 83% of the matter in the universe is dark matter and 17% is ordinary matter,' said Reg. 'And the LHC has actually created it, isn't that something?'

Then, matter-of-factly he said, 'I see you've been bumping off some retards again, haven't you?'

'They had it coming,' I replied, 'Anyway have you seen the latest crime statistics, they're well down, that's got to be a good thing hasn't it?'

'Like I told you before, be careful, you only need to slip up once and we'll both be under suspicion.'

A month went by and Prue and I were celebrating my 60th birthday at the bungalow, I was now officially an old age pensioner, drawing my works pension. With the money from the house we decided to treat ourselves to a conservatory at the back and also a cruise for a fortnight, I was missing the printing, though.

There was a news item on the tele, it was about the so-called vigilante and how he was evading capture. The Detective Chief Inspector issued an embarrassed statement saying he was using all the means at h s disposal to bring the culprit to book, but he just had nothing to go by.

Where we lived now was a virtual crime-free area so I didn't have to go out searching for retards. That was until the builder who was erecting my conservatory was telling me about the local kids vandalising his premises in Betswy Coed:

That night, when Prue was in bed, I materialised inside the builder's yard to catch a group of kids caught in the act of smashing some double-glazed units.

'Nothing too harsh,' I thought, as I strolled up to one kid who was wielding a metal bar. I took hold of his hand and snapped a finger off, then I did the same with the rest of his mates. I threw the severed fingers into the trashcan near the office. I decided to materialize into the four-dimensional universe, just outside the gate.

There were screams and yelps from the kids as they all hopped around shaking their hands, blood pouring from them. 'Fuck me, what's happened to my hand!' yelled one. 'Christ it hurts,' yelled another. I dematerialised again to reappear in my lounge. Pleased with my night's work I went upstairs to bed.

Meanwhile one of the parents of the little darlings had phoned the police, two constables arrived ten minutes later, followed by an ambulance, the rest of the kids had been taken to Accident and Emergency, by ambulance or by their parents. After treatment the group were interviewed by the two policemen.

'Where were you when the er, accident took place,' said one officer.

'We were just playing in the builder's yard,' said one.

'Oh, yes, we've had lots of complaints about vandalism from the owner of that yard. You weren't doing anything you shouldn't were you?'

'No mister.'

'So, let me get this straight, you were all 'playing' and all of a sudden you all lost a finger, you didn't trap your hands did you?'

'No mister,' they all chorused.

'Anybody see anything unusual?' asked the officer.

'Yes, I did,' said one of the kids, 'I saw a funny blue light near the gate.'

The policeman's brain clicked into gear, 'Ron,' he said turning towards his companion, 'That report about the decapitations in Walford, didn't one of the witnesses describe seeing a strange blue light there?'

'Yes that's right, what are you suggesting, that there's some connection between the two events?'

'I suppose I am. I'm going to get on to Walford headquarters right away,' said the officer.

When they got back to the station the officer phoned up Walford with his report. The message was conveyed to DI Harrison straight away.

The next day saw DI Harrison down at the small police station in Betswy Coed. The first thing he did was to bring the kids in for questioning, they all exhibited their bandaged hands, and one of them told him about the blue light he had seen near the gate.

Next was a visit to the scene of the crime, it didn't take long for an officer to find the severed fingers in the trashcan.

'This is impossible,' said one of the policemen, 'How could all the fingers have been collected like this without somebody being seen?'

DI Harrison turned towards his fellow officer, 'This is just like the Mugabe case, the severed finger and everything.'

'What are you going to do, boss?' said his companion.

'I'm going to arrange a meeting with the CIA and M15, there has to be a connection somewhere, I'm afraid our vigilante has struck again.'

By now the builder's yard was crawling with CID and the kids had been pulled in for questioning along with the builder himself, who luckily had a cast iron alibi as to his whereabouts on the night of the incident, he had been in the pub and at least a dozen witnesses could corroborate his story.

Upon returning to headquarters DI Harrison had a visit from Agent Rothwell.

'We have a basic similarity between the three events, Mugabe's severed finger and the blue light seen by the youth in the park, here we have several severed fingers and the same blue light,' said a mystified DI Harrison.

'But, as usual, we don't have a positive identification of the perpetrator,' said Agent Rothwell, 'We've got tons of evidence but no worthwhile leads.'

'I'm sending a report to the CIA, to Panetta in America,' said DI Harrison.

The newspapers got hold of the story and speculated wildly. IS THE VIGILANTE AN ALIEN? Screamed one of the reputable editions. BLUE LIGHT THE ONLY TRACE OF VIGILANTE said another.

The article read:

Reports from a leaked police source have stated that the five children (all with severed fingers) were attacked by the same thing that has been responsible for the decapitations recently. Witnesses have reported seeing a blue light near the incidents. As yet the perpetrator remains a mystery. Police have unofficially stated that they are nowhere near apprehending him, or IT.

A frustrated DI Harrison was hauled before his Detective Chief Inspector, 'What's going on Harrison?' said the DCI 'This so-called vigilante is running rings around us, and I'm not having it!'

'I can assure you sir, I'm doing everything humanly possible to make an arrest, but we don't have any leads at all.'

'Well, I'm giving you three DIs to work on the case with you, so I'm expecting some results, is that clear?'

'Yes sir,' said DI Harrison humbly.

The builder had nearly finished the conservatory and I was having a chat to him. 'How's things down at the yard?' I said.

'Oh, couldn't be better,' he replied. 'Since the er, 'incident' things have been much better it's a treat to go down there and find everything just as you've left it.'

CHAPTER 35

That night the phone rang. It was Reg.

'You know why I'm phoning don't you?" he said.

'Yes, I know,' I replied, 'You're going to tell me off again aren't you?'

"Damn right I am, why can't you materialise back in your lounge instead of at the scene of the crime, that way they won't see the blue shift that you're showing all and sundry!'

'OK, I'll bear that in mind next time,' I replied.

'There'd better not be a next time,' said Reg and he slammed the phone down.

'I love you, too,' I said to the dead phone. I couldn't help the grin on my face.

I was becoming a regular at the pub down the road and got friendly with the regulars who all wanted to put the world to rights.

'If you ask me those little gits deserved what they got,' said one.

'I see their mothers are keeping their little darlings indoors since it happened,' said another.

'I don't have a clue who this vigilante feller is, but he'd doing all right by me, I see the crime figures are at the lowest they've been since records began,' stated the landlord.

I treated myself to an extra pint and grinned inwardly.

The conservatory was finished at last and I looked forward to having a few whiskies and tonic in it.

The girls came to visit for the weekend and the bungalow was filled full of the grandchildren's laughter.

It was soon time for Prue and I to go on the cruise. Prue enjoyed it but I didn't, it was too much like being imprisoned in a floating hotel. We visited a few places like Madeira and Casablanca. But I suppose visiting the centre of the Galaxy and the Pliades took some beating.

In parliament the subject of the vigilante was brought up for discussion, a small majority came out in support of the perpetrator citing the reduction in general crime and vandalism.

That night on the BBC's programme 'Question Time' one member of the public posed the question. 'The vigilante, friend or foe?' This led to a lively debate amongst the audience with one panelist stating that the vigilante was 'cleaning up the streets, and good luck to him.'

One newspaper had a survey done and 90% of the readership voiced support for the vigilante.

I was dematerialising about once a week paying visits to various areas in and around Manchester, that was when I became suspicious of one activity in particular . . . .

CHAPTER 36

I was strolling in Longsight one evening after dark when I came across a group of Arabs frozen in the act of unloading fertilizer from the boot of a car and carrying it into a terraced house. The front door was wide open so I stepped in. There, in the lounge, were more Arabs gathered around something on the table. It was clearly a homemade bomb of some sort, complete with a timer and detonator. The timer was set for 12 o'clock, it was now 8 o'clock. I studied the bomb for a few minutes and advanced the timer to five minutes past 8. I then materialised myself back into the street well away from the red brick terraced house. Five minutes ticked by and all of a sudden there was a tremendous explosion, blasting the windows out of the house. Some of the Arabs were in the small hallway and were caught in a fireball which belched out into the street.

The doors of the neighbouring houses were flung open and people came out onto the pavement. 'Did you see what happened?' said one lady.

'It was an explosion,' I replied. 'It's blasted out the windows and doors.' The house was now well ablaze. Someone called the fire brigade, and then minutes later, they arrived and started hosing down the house.

It was time for me to make a quick exit, so I walked into a neighbouring alleyway and transposed myself back to the bungalow.

The next day the Daily Mail led with the story: BOMB FACTORY DISASTER IN TERRACED HOUSE the article read:

Last night in Longsight, Manchester a suspected bomb factory was exposed as police sifted through the debris. The police found several bags of fertilizer and various timing devices and fuses. Apparently the bomb that the Arabs were working on went off prematurely, killing seven of the occupants of the terraced house and severely burning two others. Eye witnesses reporting seeing a strange blue light at the scene. There is speculation that the notorious vigilante could have had something to do with the incident.

Meanwhile at police headquarters:

'The whole thing smells of the vigilante,' said DI Harrison to his assembled companions, 'the blue light again, and how could he have got in and triggered the bomb's mechanism? It just doesn't make sense.'

'And where did he get his intelligence from, boss,' said one of the group.

'M15 have been suspecting this group for ages,' said DI Harrison.

'Could there have been a leakage of information?' said another.

'Possibly, but it still comes down to the fact that he's almost invisible, the blue light is his Achillies heel.'

M15 visited the offices of DI Harrison the next day. Agent Rothwell was visibly shaken by the whole affair, 'If it was a leak in the system, then one of my men knows who the vigilante is,' he said.

'Maybe we have to get pro-active,' said DI Harrison.

'What do you mean?' said Agent Rothwell.

'Well we could put it around that something naughty is going down and then lie in wait and trap the bastard. Just let me think on it and I'll let you know.'

It was about 12 at night when I decided to transport myself into DI Harrison's office, just to see what the opposition was up to. There were still officers working late and there on the chalkboard were the outlines of DI Harrison's plan to trap me red handed. He was going to publish in the paper the bogus story of a little retard terrorising the neighbourhood where he lived. As soon as I took the bait he would swamp the area with police officers and get me bang to rights.

Two days later, sure enough, there appeared in the paper the case of the yob terrorising the neighbourhood where he lived. I took the bait and transposed myself into the false address where the kid lived.

When I got there the youngster was playing on an X-box, with him were two plains-clothed policemen. I casually walked over to the first officer and took out of my pocket a pre-written note which read: *To DI Harrison, you'll have to get up early to catch me*. I popped it into the officer's top pocket.

Back in the three dimensional world the policeman felt a tug on his pocket and looked down to find the note there which had appeared as if by magic, he read it and immediately reported it to his superior.

'What the hell's going on here,' exclaimed DI Harrison, 'shit, shit, shit. He's having us for a bunch of wankers, he's running rings around us.' He sent the note to forensics and went to the pub for a pint (or two).

I felt sorry for DI Harrison, the poor bloke was having a nightmare and still getting nowhere with his enquiries. It was when I was thinking about this that a seed of an idea came into my mind, what if I could help him solve some of the other cases he was working on. That would cheer him up no end. I resolved to pay his office a visit to see what I could find, it would do no harm to have a look see.

At 12 that night when Prue was fast asleep in bed, I transported myself to the DI's office There were a couple of officers caught in the act of working. I walked over to the whiteboard, it was full of information, and had the photographs of four young girls who were all presumed missing. A report on the case was half open on Harrison's desk. Nobody was near me so I thumbed through the report, apparently the four girls had vanished without trace from various places in Lancashire over the past two months, nobody knew if they were dead or alive. Each case seemed to be connected. All the usual suspects had been questioned, but there were no leads.

On the other whiteboard was a series of photographs to do with the mayhem I had caused, photos of the Gooch

Street Gang massacre and so on. I noted with satisfaction the amount of question marks shown on the board, yes, there were definitely no leads here. No wonder DI Harrison was going bonkers, he had two unsolved serious crimes on his plate. I resolved to do all I could to help him solve the case of the missing girls. But where to start?

CHAPTER 37

The next day I got in the car and went to the library in Betsy Coed, there I sifted through the computer data of the newspapers, anything I could find on the disappearance of the girls. Apparently all the crimes had been committed at or after midnight when the girls had been coming home from a night out with friends at various places in Lancashire two of them had disappeared in Manchester all had gone missing on a Saturday night. It had been as if they had disappeared off the face of the Earth. There were no immediate suspects.

That night after 12 I transposed myself to Deansgate in Manchester, it was 'chucking out' time from the many bars and pubs, and the place was heaving with girls and boys all looking for taxis to take them home. I strolled around looking for anything suspicious. I drew a blank. 'God, this is like looking for a needle in a haystack,' I thought to myself.

I went out for the next three Saturdays looking for anything that might help with DI Harrison's case. But nothing showed up. Until the fourth Saturday night came along: I was strolling casually along Princess Street when I spotted a car that had pulled up along the kerbside a young girl, on her own, was frozen in the act of getting in the rear seat. I noticed it wasn't a taxi. 'Probably it's Dad come to pick her up,' I thought, 'but why did she get in the rear seat, if she knew the driver she would surely get in the front. I took the number of the car just to be on the safe side. I circled the car and got a good eyeful of the driver and the girl, I felt it in my water, something was not quite right, the driver looked as shifty as a fox on the hunt for chickens.

Two days went by, and the morning paper's headline article blazed ANOTHER GIRL MISSING FROM MANCHESTER. The article was about a young girl last seen on her own after saying goodbye to her friends on Princess Street Manchester, this was the last that had been seen of her and that police were tying it in with the case of the other four girls disappearances. No CCTV footage was available. There was a photo of the missing girl.

'It was her! The girl that was getting in the car on Saturday. What to do now? I had to think, fast, I had the car's number but that was no good. I needed an address of the owner. I also knew it was a black Ford Focus. The only place I could think of to get the address was the DVLC in Swansea.

I waited until one o'clock in the morning for Prue to fall asleep and then transported myself to Swansea. The place was deserted save for a lone security guard. I climbed the stairs into the main offices where the computers were, I switched on the one nearest to me. I entered the Reg. number of the Ford Focus. Within less than a minute the address of the owner flashed up on the screen. Thomas Crowe, Highbury Farm, Derbyshire. Bingo!

The next night I crept out of bed next to a slumbering Prue, and transported myself to Highbury farm.

The farmhouse was in a poor state of repair, with broken windows and hanging guttering, I almost thought it was deserted, there was no sign of the black Ford Focus. There were no lights on so I re-transported myself inside the building. There was no-one there, the place was deserted, on the dining room table where what looked like the remains of a meal and some dirty dishes. So someone was living there after all. I had a quick look round the bedrooms but they revealed nothing. Not even a knife or a gun showed up. Somewhat disheartened I transported myself back home. When I got there Prue was up brewing a cup of tea.

'Where have you been at this hour?" she said.

'Oh, I just got up for a walk, I couldn't sleep.'

'You'll catch your death of a cold walking about at this time of the morning,' she scolded. 'Come back to bed and keep me cozy,' she said with a twinkle in her eye.

The next day I didn't know what to do, should I inform DI Harrison of what I knew or should I investigate further. I decided on the latter. That night I again transported myself to the farmhouse.

This time the black Ford was outside the front door which was ajar. I slipped in. When I got into the lounge the moth eaten carpet was pulled back to reveal an open trap door in the floor. 'Of course, a cellar!" I thought to myself. I crept slowly down the steps and into the cellar. And there they were the five missing girls—they were all chained to the cellar wall while Thomas Crowe sat on a chair like a king surveying his courtiers.

'The bastard, I could waste him now and then inform the police,' I thought. But then I had a re-think and decided to let

221

DI Harrison get all the glory. I transported myself to a public phone in Castleton, Derbyshire. There I dematerialised and phoned the police.

The operator came on and I requested to be put through to the DI's office. The operator said, 'I don't think anyone will be there at this hour, but I'll put you through anyway.'

The phone rang in Harrison's office and an officer picked it up.

'I've got some information regarding the missing girls for DI Harrison,' I said. 'They're all shacked up at Highbury Farm, Derbyshire. A feller called Thomas Crowe is holding them prisoner, this is the vigilante.' I rang off and transported myself back home and got back to bed, well satisfied of my evening's work.

The officer got on the phone to DI Harrison, getting him out of bed, 'Well, it could be a hoax call I suppose but it won't do any harm to take a look,' said DI Harrison. 'I want two squads plus the Armed Response Unit. We'll meet up at headquarters for a briefing before we go in.'

Soon there was a team of officers assembled in the headquarters office plus the ARU, DI Harrison was just finishing, 'Remember this guy is a farmer so he's bound to have a shotgun on him.'

There was a shotgun alright, Crowe carried it about with him wherever he went.

Soon the police had surrounded Highbury Farm and a group of them were ready to go in, one of them had a metal ram for breaking down the front door. Then they were ready. SMASH! The door was battered down, and the police rushed in screaming, 'armed police, do not resist, police, police.

They needn't have bothered, Crowe was fast asleep in bed when they burst in, they got him up and sat him down on a chair in the lounge. 'Do you know anything about the missing girls in the paper, Mr. Crowe?'

'No officer,' Crowe lied.

"We have a warrant to search the premises sir,' said one of the officers. 'So if you're hiding anything you'd better tell us now.'

'No, nothing, officer.'

The police searched high and low but came across nothing.

'Tell me Mr. Crowe, does this place have a cellar?' said DI Harrison.

'No, officer.'

DI Harrison went over to the rug and pulled it back, revealing the trap door in the floor.

'Hello, what have we got here then?' he said to his colleagues, 'no cellar hey. Have you got the key to this mortise lock Mr. Crowe?'

'It's on the bureau,' said Crowe.

The policeman found the key and opened the trap door, there was a light on in the cellar, he went down the steps and discovered the five girls who were all sobbing with relief, the keys to the shackles were hanging on the wall well out of reach of the girls. The policeman soon had them free and one of them collapsed into his arms with relief.

Turning to Crowe DI Harrison said, 'Thomas Crowe I'm arresting you on suspicion of kidnap, anything you might say . . . .' and so on.

The girls climbed up the stairs from the cellar and one of them launched herself at Crowe kicking and scratching. The police let her get it out of her system for a few minutes before dragging her off. Two ambulances arrived to take the girls for a check-up at the hospital. Crowe was handcuffed and shoved into the police van to be taken to the lock-up.

'What was he intending doing to the poor sods,' said one officer to DI Harrison.

'Dunno, mate,' said Harrison, 'looks like he was keeping them as a sort of trophy. One of those girls has been in that cellar for nearly a year now. Where's the officer that took the call from the informant?'

'It was me sir,' said one of the officers stepping forward.

'So tell me officer,' said the DI 'what makes you think it was the vigilante who informed?'

'Well, he just said so, he signed off and said this is the vigilante.'

'So we have a benevolent vigilante now do we?' said DI Harrison.

CHAPTER 38

A month later Crowe appeared in court and was sentenced to prison indefinitely pending psychiatric reports. It was brought up in the court that the vigilante had played a vital part in the capture of Crowe by providing the key lead to the police.

BBC's Panorama devoted a whole programme to the vigilante with the title, VIGILANTE, FRIEND OR FOE?

That night Reg rang me up and said, 'At least now you're doing some good, I suppose.

That left me with a warm feeling inside.

Unofficially DI Harrison didn't have the compunction to apprehend the vigilante anymore, after all crime figures were down and there was always the chance that the vigilante might help in some way with his outstanding cases.

The five girls (who were beauties by the way) were interviewed on Breakfast Time on GTV. They all chorused 'Vigilante we love you' and giggled their pretty little arses off. None of them had been molested by Crowe who had admitted to being impotent at his trial. They had been incarcerated just to be 'looked at' by him. DI Harrison was correct, they were nothing more than human trophies to him. There was a warning to the public: Don't get in unmarked cars, make sure that the taxi is displaying the correct details.

DI Harrison was eternally grateful to the vigilante and I helped him with a further two cases, one was a repeat burglar and the other was a car thief that was using violent assault on his victims to get the keys to their cars. Both got good meaty sentences.

'How does he know who to target?' queried the DI, it's as if he has carte blanch to all our information.'

Harrison was completely mystified not knowing, of course, that I was in and out of his office like one of his own officers. And reading all his briefs on the cases he was investigating. We were getting to be quite a team.

CHAPTER 39

Reg and I were dematerialising together about once a month, going to fabulous places in the Universe. We went to mainly G-type stars within our own galaxy that had planetary systems. There were a huge variety of life forms but no intelligent life like on Earth, it was just a matter of time before we would come across humanoids like us. We had seen that there were a race of superior beings to us at the centre of the Galaxy, and in the constellation of Orion.

It was a beautiful summer day and I decided to take a stroll down the lane to the pub. All the locals were in, chatting away, so I joined them, the conversation turned towards one of them, George Smith, who was having trouble with a problem family that had moved in next door to him. They had been housed by the local housing association, and were shouting abuse at him and his wife and kids. The father of the family was on sickness benefit but didn't seem too sick to be standing at the gate swearing and cursing at everyone who came in earshot. The mother was a big fat piece with a gob to go with it. There were six kids all running amok in the neighbourhood.

I asked George where he lived, just matter-of-factly. 'Rosemary Lane,' he replied.

I decided to pay the family a visit. I waited until midnight and transported myself into the kitchen of number 12 Rosemary Lane. First I stacked the chairs on top of the table then opened all the doors of the kitchen cabinets along with the drawers. Then I transported myself back home and went to bed.

The next morning, when they got up, the family were met by the disturbance in the kitchen, 'Which one of you bloody kids has done this?' said mother.

'Not us mam,' they chorused.

'Well, I think one of you did it, I'll tan your arses if it was any of you wot did it.'

'Honest mam, it wasn't us.'

That midnight I transported myself again and did exactly the same only this time I opened the drawers and tipped the contents all over the kitchen floor. Then I went into the lounge and pushed the sofa and armchairs into the centre of the room. I then transported myself home.

The next morning Mam was going berserk, 'I'm telling you, you little bastards I'll kill the one that's responsible for all this.'

"It wasn't us,' the kids repeated, then one of them said, 'Maybe we've got a ghost, one of them polterg . . . . thingies.'

'I don't believe in ghosts,' retorted mam, 'It's bullshit believing that they exist.'

I waited until the afternoon as Prue went out to the shops and transported myself to the house of the problem family. It was time to up the ante. The mother was sprawled out in the lounge watching cartoons on the tele. I pushed the armchair opposite her across the room. Then I left.

Seen from the mother's point of view the armchair appeared to move across the room and come to rest on the opposite side.

'Jesus, what was that?' she exclaimed.

The husband entered the room, 'what's up with you woman, you've gone as white as a sheet,' he said.

'I've just seen the armchair shoot across the room on its own, that's what,' she said. 'Christ, maybe the kids were right, we have got a ghost.'

'Rubbish,' said the father, 'There's no such thing, I'll make you a nice cuppa, you'll be alright then.'

I let a day go by and visited the family again at midnight, this time I took a red aerosol spray with me, I entered the lounge and sprayed 'GET OUT' in large letters over the fireplace.

That morning the woman entered her lounge, saw the lettering and screamed, fit to bust. Dad came rushing down the stairs and looked in disbelief at the wall, 'Where the hell did that come from?' he exclaimed.

'I don't know, something put it there in the night, I'm telling you, this place is haunted.' This time dad agreed.

I waited until tea time before transporting myself again, the family were all sat around the kitchen table eating their meal. I opened the drawer in one of the units and threw all the cutlery all over the room.

The lot of them crapped themselves, 'Right, that's it, I'm down at the housing tomorrow and getting us out of here, I don't want to spent another night in this house,' spluttered mam.

The woman was first in the queue at the housing association's office the next morning.

'You see, the problem is, is that it's common for people to invent ghosts when they want to move house,' said the housing officer.

'Listen, you pen-pushing bastard, I'm telling you that house is haunted!' exclaimed mam, she was joined by her husband who had just been to the bookies to place a bet.

'Look I've seen it with my very own eyes. I've seen cutlery flying across the room,' said dad.

The official said, 'Well, the best we can do is come and see what's happening at the property.'

'Look all you want, you'll soon see I'm telling you the truth,' said mam.

It was nine o'clock the next morning and the housing officer was visiting the family—I decided to put on a good show, I flung open all the doors and drawers in the kitchen for starters then piled all the chairs in one corner of the room. Then I went home.

The officer was scared out of his wits by the goings on at the house.

Two days later the family was offered another property in a rundown area of Betsy Coed. 'Good, they'll be living next door to their own kind this time, not decent law-abiding folk like George Smith,' I thought to myself.

So that was it, job done! Another satisfied customer.

CHAPTER 40

That weekend I was down at Reg's visiting him while Marcia was out, 'You know, we've been to lots of places together but never come across intelligent life in human form, except for Merope where you saw human-type beings,' said Reg. 'I think we ought to go there and make contact with them.'

'How?' I asked.

'Well, we could dematerialise on the planet's surface once we get there.'

'How would we breathe,' I said.

'I'm assuming the planet has an atmosphere rich in oxygen, so we should be able to breathe quite comfortably,' Reg replied.

'OK, then, let's give it a try,' I said.

Soon we were looking down on the planet on the far Merope, two moons hung in the sky, the blue sun was just setting. We then landed on the planet's surface on the beautiful beach, three humanoids were caught in the act of pulling their boat up the shoreline, presumably they had been fishing.

'Right,' said Reg, 'let's give it a go.' With that he dematerialised. I followed suit, 'it's OK,' he said, 'Come on in the water's fine.'

Breathing was easy, the atmosphere was oxygen rich just as Reg had forecast. So we walked slowly up the beach to where the three humanoids stood, they looked alarmed at seeing us and crowded together.

We walked slowly up the beach towards them. Reg held out his hands in front of him, 'Hold out your hands,' he said.

I did the same and held out my hands at waist level, palms upward. The humanoids did the same, we carried on until we were two feet away from them. They had no noses just two nostrils set wide apart on their faces, their skin was translucent and you could easily see the veins below the surface, they were dressed in a sort of loin cloth type garment. I looked into huge coal-black eyes. Then an amazing thing happened, we all touched hands, theirs were icy cold and very smooth.

'We ought to say something,' I said.

Reg took a deep breath and said, 'We are from planet Earth.'

The tallest humanoid opened his mouth and said something in a delightful sing-song voice.

As we had no idea what each of us were talking about, Reg smoothed out a patch of sand with his foot and picked up a stick. He then drew a diagram of the solar system and pointed to the third planet from the sun. The humanoid did the same thing and pointed to the fifth planet from Merope.

They then indicated that we should follow them up a rough path into the dense jungle. After about five minutes we came to a clearing with five mud-built huts in it—a fire was burning in the centre of the small village, there were several large logs around the campfire and the humanoids beckoned us to sit, they were all chattering away in their beautiful sing-song dialect. Some children came out of the huts to look at us, filled with curiosity. The tallest humanoid picked up a stick and drew several rectangles with what looked like windows inside them and what looked like roads running amongst them.

'It looks like he's drawing a city,' said Reg in awe.

'I think so too,' I replied.

'We've been here for nearly two hours,' said Reg, 'Marcia will be wondering where I am.

We decided to transport ourselves home to return at a later date.

Luckily, when Reg got in Marcia was still out. 'Here's my theory of what we have seen,' said Reg. that race of humanoids were a tribe of people just like you would find on earth in deepest Africa. They are a race of primitive people, but I'm sure we'll find a more sophisticated culture if we look long and hard enough. But that would mean staying for at least a couple of days.

'I know,' I said, maybe we could say that we are going to CERN in Geneva again, that would give us all the time we would need to explore the planet.'

And so we agreed to tell the girls we were going to Geneva for three days on the following week. The next week soon came round and we had our bags packed as if we were catching a flight, instead we met up at the bungalow and drove to the car park in the wool mill near Penmachno. There we dematerialised ourselves to the fifth planet of Merope. We landed back on the beautiful beach with the blue sun shining down. We located the path and walked to the village, I found that I was breathing harder than usual. 'That's because we are in a world that is bigger than Earth and has a higher G-force, we weigh heavier here than we do at home,' said Reg.

'Trust him, the flippin' know it all,' I thought.

When we got in sight of the village the children rushed to meet us, chattering excitedly, followed by several adult humanoids who indicated that we should sit down near the fire on the logs, which we did, one of them, which we perceived to be a female of the species, brought out two cups filled with what tasted like guava juice. We drank and put the cups down. Reg picked a stick out of the fire and smoothed the ground with his hand, he then drew a picture of the city as the humanoid had done then he indicated walking with his fingers. The tallest humanoid, who was clearly the leader, squatted down saying something in a lilting sing-song voice, he stretched out his arm and indicated walking in the dirt with his long slender fingers.

That was it, we were on our way, but not before we had been given some fruit to eat, which tasted delicious. The humanoid ushered us towards a path that lead out of the clearing, soon we came to a metalled road, he stretched out his arm and pointed down the road and again indicated walking with his fingers. There he left us to our own devices.

We must have walked at least two miles down the road, breathing heavily in the higher g-force. Then Reg said, 'Look at that," and pointed ahead. Out of the mist, the outline of the city appeared, with what seemed like skyscrapers reaching delicately up to the sky. As we neared the city we could see flying machines flitting to and fro from one building to the next, 'That's their mode of transport,' I said.

'Yeah,' said Reg, 'they use the sky like we use the roads, I would say they are more advanced than us wouldn't you?'

'I agree,' I replied.

Just then a four-wheeled vehicle came humming down the road. It pulled up and the humanoid in it looked at us for a minute then carried on towards the city.

'So, they use the roads as well as the sky,' said Reg.

'Perhaps he's going to raise the alarm,' I said.

'Probably.'

We journeyed on until we came to the outskirts of the city. More of the four-wheeled vehicles put in an appearance. Then a small convoy of vehicles drove towards us, stopped, and the passengers got out. 'Put out your hands,' said Reg. We both stretched out our arms and turned our palms upward. The occupants of the vehicles did the same. We touched hands. These humanoids were dressed in a

237

kind of toga like the roman emperors used to wear in our world, Reg's theory was right on the nail (as usual). These humanoids were more indicative of the civilisation on this world.

They then indicated towards one of the vehicles and opened the door clearly wanting us to get in, which we did. The vehicle hummed down the road towards the centre of the city. 'Clearly powered by electricity,' said Reg. We pulled up outside the tallest skyscraper, it's graceful columns reaching up into the sky, the flying craft buzzing around it like a swarm of bees. We were ushered in, everything in the building was diamond white, the walls, the desks at which the humanoids sat and the floors, the chairs, everything. We were steered towards one of the walls, which opened seamlessly to reveal a lift. We entered. The lift purred towards the top floor of the skyscraper, where we were treated to a wonderful panoramic view of the city.

A group of humanoids were waiting for us, one of them wore a scarlet red toga unlike the others who wore white. 'Obviously the head honcho,' I whispered to Reg.

'Yeah, quite a reception committee,' he observed.

They indicated towards two of the pristine white chairs for us to be seated. The humanoid in red went over to his desk and produced what looked like a lap-top computer. It projected a hologram of the Merope system six inches above his desk. He indicated the fifth planet with a slender tapering finger and said something in his own tongue. Then he projected our own familiar system, Reg stood up and indicated the third planet from the sun and said, 'Earth.' The figure in red tilted his head quizzickly obviously not understanding. One of the other humanoids came over and tapped on the desk with what looked like a pen. Reg and I looked at each other in puzzlement until Reg said excitedly, 'It's the prime numbers, he's tapping out the prime numbers!'

Reg rapped on the desk with his knuckles answering the message by tapping out the prime numbers. This caused a ripple of excitement and they all started chattering at once in their sing-song voices. Then another of the humanoids came over to where we sat and produced a slim rod of metal which he put in front of our faces he then indicated lip movement with his mouth.

'He wants you to say something,' I said, 'it must be a microphone of some sort.'

Reg said, 'What'll I say?'

'Anything,' I replied, 'try the Lord's Prayer.'

Reg intoned, 'Our Father which art in heaven . . . .' and so on. As he spoke the hologram produced symbols in the air which we guessed was the alien's writing. Then the computer spoke to the humanoids in their own language. One of them spoke into the microphone and the computer spoke in a monotone, 'Our father which art in heaven . . . . !'

'It's a sampler,' said Reg excitedly. 'It samples each language and then translates.'

Sure enough the computer intoned, 'What is your planet called?'

239

'Earth,' I said into the microphone.

'Earth,' said the computer.

Then the alien in red started to type data into the computer, mathematical symbols flashed up in the air.

'Ah, maths,' said Reg, 'the universal language.' The humanoids then produced a sheet of paper and a writing instrument.

'How did you get here, where is your ship?' the computer asked.

Reg wrote on the paper the maths that appertained to the fifth dimension. More maths appeared in the hologram. Reg wrote some more in reply. As this was going on I thought 'We are actually conversing with an alien race, this is incredible, the whole of planet Earth should know about this. But how to tell them without spilling the beans of Reg's true theory?'

We conversed through the humanoids computer for another hour telling them all about our race and where we had got to in space exploration and so on. Just then one of them came into the room with a tray on which were placed drinking vessels and a jug, the alien poured out an amber liquid into two of the cups and motioned for us to drink. It tasted like the best Chardonnay ever. The aliens couldn't understand how we had got to their planet without a ship, until Reg showed them how using maths as a language.

'Do you have linear accelerators on your planet?' I queried.

'Yes we do,' the computer replied.

'Have you produced the strange particle that we call the Higgs boson?'

'Yes,' came the answer, 'Many seasons ago.'

We were ushered to a doorway into another room where one of the aliens put his hands on the side of his head to indicate sleep. There were four beds in the pure white room. I lay on one of them and tried to go to sleep, but my mind was racing, I could see that Reg was having the same problem. 'How far advanced do you think they are Reg?'

'I'd say about 300 years further than us,' he replied. 'And they still haven't discovered the fifth dimension, incredible isn't it?'

'Well, they certainly have now. I suppose they will visit Earth someday.'

Two hours went past and then one of the humanoids came into the room and opened a seamless door in the wall and beckoned us over to a small shower cubicle which we gratefully used. Then he motioned us to follow him and led us into what only can be described as a banqueting room. There were tables full of strange fruits and whitemeat that tasted like chicken. There was more of the amber wine, we were seated at a large table at one end of the room with the alien in the red toga.

'They certainly know how to throw a party, don't they?' Reg whispered in my ear. There was a strange lilting sound in

241

the air coming from nowhere in particular, I reckoned it was their music that was playing, 'I wonder what they would think of Lady Ga Ga,' I thought.

The evening went well and soon we were indicating sleep to one of the aliens, who showed us back into the bedroom.'

I was soon well away on the comfortable bed, with Reg snoring away opposite me.

The next morning we got up, showered and were brought a breakfast of what looked and tasted like porridge. We were then showed into the boardroom to continue our conversation via the computer. We were told that their planet was called Leon and that they were the Leonis. We found out that they had a democratic system of government and that they lived on average of 150 Earth years. They had industry and commerce and had music and the arts and no crime to speak of although some of their high-ranking officials had been known to take a bribe or two. There was no mention of religion.

So I asked, 'Do you believe in God?'

'God? What is God?' voiced the computer, 'We have no God, there is only us.'

'That's a smack in the eye for all the religious fanatics out there,' I thought, 'If God exists surely an intelligent race like this would also believe?'

That afternoon we went on a tour of one of their factories which produced the flying machines that we had seen flitting around in the city, in fact we were transported there in one of them. The factory operated almost exactly like our car production sites on Earth, with robotic machines doing the donkey work. We also visited one of their hospitals, although sickness and disease was very rare amongst them, the hospitals could perform minor miracles like limb replacement and organ plus parts of the brain replacement. That evening we were the guests of honour at another sumptuous banquet. The most intriguing visit was to one of their research centres where they had a high powered radio source transmitting a signal into outer space sending a message that they were here, they told us it had been transmitting for 450 years with no reply. They had explored all of their neighbouring planets.

The next day we told the humaroids that our visit was nearly over and that we would have to be thinking about going home. I felt a strange affection for this race of gentle, hospitable people that we had visited. We decided that we would let them observe us when we dematerialised.

That evening it was time to go, so we stood in the middle of the banqueting room surrounded by the humanoids and thought hard about the theory and then my car at the wool mill, the blue shift surrounded us and we were transposed back into the car.

CHAPTER 41

"Phew, that certainly was a strange three days, Dick,' said Reg.

'You can say that again,' I said, putting the car into gear and moving off, 'We have to make the scientific community on earth aware of the Leonis somehow.'

'I agree,' said Reg, 'Just let me think on it for a while.'

I dropped Reg off and headed for home, thinking of the last few days on an alien planet.

Prue was waiting for me at the door as I drove up the drive, I gave her a big hug and a kiss as I entered the hallway, 'How did you get on?' she said.

'Oh, great,' I replied, 'the LHC has proved that dark matter - and faster than light neutrinos - exist.'

'Fancy a drink?' said Prue.

'Not half,' I replied. I thought of that old saying, 'wherever you may wander there's no place like home.'

I sat down feeling happy and contented with life.

The next day I received a phone call from Reg: 'I know what we can do, we can inform SETI (Search for Extraterrestrial Intelligence). They will soon find out about the Merope system and should pick up some radio sources from them. The mission of the SETI Institute is to explore, understand and explain the origin, nature and prevalence of life in the Universe. Founded in November 1984, the SETI Institute began operations on February 1, 1985. Today it employs over 150 scientists, educators and support staff. Research at the Institute is anchored by two centres. Dr. Jill Tarter leads the Centre for SETI Research. Dr. David Morrison is the Director for the Carl Sagan Centre for the Study of Life in the Universe. Edna DeVorre leads the Centre for Education and Public outreach. I intend to contact Jill Tarter, she's the main man.'

'OK, Reg I wish you good luck, please let me know how you get on,' I said.

Reg sent an E-mail to Dr. Tarter, It read: Dear Dr. Tarter, I am contacting you to ask you to turn your attention to the Merope System in the Plaiedes cluster, there you will find an earth-like planet called Leon, plus another ten planets with gas giants like our own solar system, I have reason to believe that life as we know it exists there. You should be able to pick up some sort of signal from the system. Regards Reginald Stein.

Dr. Tarter sent a reply: Dear Mr. Stein, as you may or may not know, here at SETI we have hundreds of likely sources at which we turn our detectors. The Merope system is a young blue star and is highly unlikely to have developed life, let alone intelligent life. May I ask why you have turned your attention to this particular star—Jill Tarter.

245

Reg replied: Dear Dr. Tarter, I appreciate that you are busy on other projects, but I emplore you to turn your detectors to the Merope system, I know you will find signs that an intelligent race of life exists there, please don't ask me how I know, I just know it! I would stake my reputation on it.—Regards Reginald Stein.

Dr. Tarter: Dear Mr. Stein, because of your reputation within the scientific community, and only because of that, here at SETI we shall do as you ask. This is to let you know that we shall aim our radio telescopes at the star Merope in exactly two day's time. I have sent you my phone number should you have any enquiries—Jill Tarter.

Reg phoned me up with the exciting news: 'They are going to try to detect signals from Merope in two days,' he said excitedly.

'Oooh, that's great,' I exclaimed, 'better hold the front page then.'

Two days later SETI turned its attention towards the Merope system, straightaway detecting a faint radio source which was immediately obvious: It was a series of pulses which corresponded to the prime numbers.

'My God, the man was right, we have discovered extraterrestrial intelligent life!' exclaimed Dr. Tarter. The room erupted in cheers and Scientists were hugging each other and backslapping their workmates, 'I have to contact Dr. Morrison and Reginald Stein at once.' She said, 'Oh yes, and NASA, they will be interested to turn the Hubble

Telescope on the system.' She could hardly dial the telephone numbers in her excitement.

Reg was waiting by the telephone. Soon Dr. Tarter phoned him with the news: 'My dear Mr. Stein, you were correct in your assumptions that intelligent life exists in the Merope system. What happens now is that we shall send a reply, though the star is 410 light years from us. Congratulations Mr. Stein. We shall be meeting the Press as soon as possible.'

Reg phoned me with the news. 'It worked, Dick,' he exclaimed SETI had found intelligent life in the Universe.'

'Congratulations, Reg, I only hope you get the recognition you deserve.'

The news went crazy—and world wide—in a matter of hours. The papers went mad with headlines like LIFE IN THE UNIVERSE, OFFICIAL, the Daily star led with LITTLE GREEN MEN CONTACT US—typical. The BBC had a special newsflash: Today SETI (Search for Extraterrestrial Intelligence) has found just that, intelligent life in the Universe, signals have been picked up from a star lying in the Pliaedies 410 Light years from Earth, Dr. Tarter the director at SETI has stated that the discovery would not have happened if it hadn't been for the well known physicist, famous for his work on the Theory of Relativity, Reginald Stein tipping them off as to the whereabouts of the planet. The Hubble Telescope is to turn its attention to the planet as soon as possible.

I phoned Reg up: 'You'll be a household name in a bit,' I said.

And sure enough he was.

The whole world and his dog wanted a piece of Reg from then on. I was kept busy organising seminars and public appearances worldwide. Of course everybody wanted to know how Reg knew about life in the Merope system he fobbed it off by saying it was 'intuition,' and that he had a 'hunch' about the planet Leon. Later on in the year of 2011 Reg was awarded the Nobel Prize in physics, and I went with him to Stockholm Sweden to collect his medal and his prize money. Who would have guessed that this idle, beer swilling, unassuming man would one day achieve what he has done. Marcia was so proud of him she was fit to bust.

CHAPTER 42

Meanwhile on the planet Leon the inhabitants were having difficulty accessing the fifth dimension. The math was proving too hard for them to comprehend, up till now only Reg could work out the equations that were necessary. We hadn't told them that all you had to do was believe in the Theory and you would be able to travel in the Universe that we call the fifth dimension.

Reg was a genius in relativistic mathematics and was so advanced that it would be hundreds of years before another fella like him would come along. He earned his Bachelor of Science (with hons) in mathematics and took up a tutorship at Kings College London, where he taught math to his adoring students.

Even Regina was proud of him, she wrote him a cursory note saying, 'I suppose all that chit-chat with your like-minded friends has paid off at last, you are truly a mad scientist.'

One weekend Reg and Marcia came to visit at the bungalow, the girls were in the kitchen washing up after our meal. Reg and I were in the lounge with a brandy each. "I've decided to take the theory one stage further,' said Reg quietly.

'Oh, yes and how's that?' I replied.

'Well, there's some maths in the Theory that make travel through time possible, I just have to finalise some of the equations and I reckon that I should be able to travel to the future or the past, but the whole situation is fraught with danger, the trouble is that the timing is a hit and miss affair and I might not get back to the present so easily,' said Reg.

'God, that's wonderful,' I said excitedly, 'just think of the potential if it's true time travel!'

'I must ask you to keep it as our secret,' Reg replied.

'Sure thing.'

Just then the girls came back into the lounge and conversation carried on in a more mundane fashion.

A week passed by and Reg phoned me: 'I have finalised the maths and I am going to attempt travel in time on Saturday.'

'Ooh, that's great,' I said excitedly, 'are you going to the future or the past?'

'The future.'

'I wish I were coming with you,' I said excitedly.

'Well, let's see how I go on and perhaps you can accompany me at another time later on. I have to go now, Marcia's coming.'

I put the phone down and thought hard about the situation, it was almost impossible to comprehend what Reg was about to do. Where in the future was he going to travel?

It was Sunday afternoon when the phone rang, it was Marcia, 'Have you seen Reg? We both went to bed and I haven't seen him since One O'clock this morning, it's twelve thirty in the afternoon now and I haven't seen hide nor hair of him.'

'Perhaps he's gone for a walk,' I replied, 'he often does that when he is working on something or other.'

'Not without telling me first.'

Alarm bells started to ring in my head. 'Just give it a few more hours,' I said, 'He's bound to turn up soon.'

'Well, I hope so,' said Marcia and rang off.

After tea that night I rang Marcia, 'Any news?'

'No, he's still missing, I'm getting worried now Dick, where the hell is he?'

'Give it till the morning and inform the police,' I replied, 'that's all I can think of.'

The next day there was still no sign of Reg. The police came round and said they would keep an eye out for him and that they would check the hospitals, etc. They comforted Marcia by telling her that it was usual for the missing person to be back usually within 48 hours. There was none of Reg's clothing missing or any personal effects like his wallet or keys and so on.

A week went by and still no sign of Reg. Marcia rang up, 'I'm sick with worry Dick, what if he's lying in a ditch somewhere?'

The police stepped up the search and went through the local area with a fine tooth comb, they drew a blank. It wasn't long before the newspapers got hold of the story. The Guardian led with: FAMOUS PHYSICIST GOES MISSING, *The world famous physicist Professor Reginald Stein has been reported missing from his home in Cheshire yesterday, nothing has been heard from him for over a week now. Police said that it was most unusual for Professor Stein to be away for so long a period of time. His devoted wife Marcia has appealed for any member of the public with information to come forward.*

I had to phone around to cancel his dates for public appearances indefinitely. Another week went by and there was still no sign of Reg. What if he is trapped in the future? I thought, the bugger might never get back!

Reg had been missing for four weeks now and me and Prue went down to Cheshire to comfort Marcia. We were all sat in the lounge when the front doorbell rang. 'I'll get it,' I said. 'It'll probably be a newspaper reporter or something.'

I opened the door and there stood Reg! 'Well I'll be . . . .' I said in astonishment.

Reg whispered, 'Just go along with whatever I say, Dick promise me, yeah?'

"Ok,' I replied, 'Glad to have you back again.' I shouted to Marcia, 'Marcia it's Reg, he's home.'

Marcia met Reg in the hallway and threw her arms around his neck, 'Where the hell have you BEEN, we've all been worried sick.'

'I think I've had some sort of amnesiac attack, I can't remember much at all apart from wandering around all over the place, then all of a sudden I remembered where I lived.'

'I told you not to work so hard, you silly man,' cried Marcia. 'Right, that does it, we're going on holiday, Dick has already cancelled your public appearances for the foreseeable future.'

'I think we'd better inform the police,' I said.

The police came round and after listening to Reg's story they recommended that he went to hospital for a check-up.

I told Marcia not to worry and that I would take Reg to A&E, besides, it would be a chance to get Reg on his own so he could tell me what really happened. We were on our way to hospital and Reg was chattering away, 'I have been caught in a state of Limbo for the past month Dick, trapped between the third and fourth dimension. I had decided to travel in time just four weeks into the future, it was a good job I chose such a relatively short space of time because I had to wait for the past to catch up with the future, what if I had gone for a hundred years or something, it doesn't bear thinking about. There must be a flaw in my mathematics I'll have to work on it some more.'

We went into the hospital and they gave Reg a thorough check-up, pronouncing him fit as the proverbial butcher's dog. When we got outside there was a small gaggle of Newsmen and the television reporters.

'Didn't take them long to latch on to us did it?' said Reg.

'You've been hot news since your 'disappearance,'' I replied.

'Professor Stein, how are you now, and where have you been for the past four weeks?' yelled one reporter.

'I'm, um, OK, and glad to be back home,' replied Reg.

"Are you going to take things easy and recuperate?' shouted another.

'I intend to go on holiday, yes,' said Reg.

We got into the car and moved off, 'I hope you don't intend doing something like this again,' I said.

"I told you, the maths just need to be perfected, so I will try again.'

'Oh, no,' I groaned.

When we got to Reg's house there was the usual crowd of reporters outside waiting for us. 'Professor Stein will issue a full Press statement in the morning, meanwhile he is now going to rest and shall be taking the telephone off the hook. So we ask you to respect that,' I addressed the group.

We went in and Marcia greeted us, 'Is he alright?' she said worriedly.

'He's fine,' I replied.

'Nothing that a good slug of brandy can't cure,' said Reg. Do you want one Dick? I presume you'll be staying overnight.'

'Yeah, I suppose so.'

CHAPTER 43

When the next day dawned the newspapers had been delivered, Reg was in the news again, the Daily Star led with the headline DID ALIENS ABDUCT TOP SCIENTIST? It was typical of them. The rest all had their own theories as to what had happened.

'It's time to address the Press,' I reminded Reg.

"OK, let them in.' Reg told the reporters to come in and led them to the front room of his spacious house. He told them that he had had a slight spell of amnesia brought on by overwork and pressure from the media and that he had been wandering around not knowing what day it was or where he was, until he suddenly remembered everything and had come straight home where he had been pronounced fit and well by the doctors.

The reporters seemed satisfied with Reg's explanation and they shuffled out to write up their stories.

Reg went into the lounge and sat his son on his knee. 'Am I glad to be home,' he said contentedly.

The next day found Reg to be on the front pages again, the stories corroborated his version of events saying that he had some sort of breakdown caused by overwork and stress.

Marcia went straight on the internet and booked a fortnight's holiday in the Bahamas. Prue and I said we would baby-sit their toddler while they were away. I got on the phone and cancelled all engagements for the next two months. Reg confided in me saying that the break would give him a chance to devote his time on the time travel aspect of his theory.

After a week I went round to Reg's to pick up his son as they were due to fly out that day. When I got the little lad home my two daughters were there, they oohd and aahd over him and played with him non-stop. All too soon the fortnight passed and it was time to take Reg's boy home, Marcia flew out of the front door and took him by the hand and gave him a big hug, 'Ooh I've missed you sooo much,' she cried.

'How did you enjoy your holiday,' I asked needlessly, because they both had healthy tans.

'It was great,' said Reg, 'But we both missed the little man something rotten.'

Marcia took the boy into the kitchen for something to eat and Reg and I went into the lounge.

'I think I've found the flaw in my maths,' Reg whispered.

'Oh, so what does that mean,' I queried.

'It means that I can time travel unhindered.'

'Please be careful, Reg. You know what happened last time,' I said.

257

'I know,' he said with a hushed voice, 'but this time I think I have perfected the equations. I intend to try it out at the first available opportunity.'

'When will you be available to meet your adoring public,' I said.

'Give it a fortnight, and we can resume normal service,' Reg replied.

'Do you still want to do the American tour,' I queried.

'Yes of course, don't forget I haven't actually been ill, you know. Do you fancy coming with me?'

'Yes I think I can, but I'll have to clear it with Prue first,' I replied.

Prue wasn't too pleased about me going to America with Reg, but grudgingly gave her consent. I spent the next day booking the hotels for our stay, we were going to do New York, Washington, Nashville, Memphis, New Orleans, Houston, Dallas, Los Angeles and finally, San Francisco. We were going to hire a car when we got there. The trip would take four weeks in total.

After a fortnight we were ready for our trip to America, Reg had not traveled in time yet saying that he couldn't afford any risks and preferred going over the mathematics time and time again. We said our goodbyes at the airport and we were off.

'I have to tell you this,' said Reg as we journeyed on the plane, 'I'm intending to take a short trip into the future of an hour or so one day while we're on our journey across America.'

'Oh, shit,' I complained, 'I hope you know what you're doing this time because it'll be me that will have to sort everything out if you go missing again.'

'Don't worry it's going to be OK this time, I'd stake my life on it,' said Reg.

CHAPTER 44

We arrived at New York for 9 a.m., jet-lagged. We went over to the car hire counter and hired a Buick, she was a beauty, an automatic, it took me about ten minutes to get used to it and soon I was happy as a pig in shit. Reg was the map-reader. We headed straight for the hotel where I had booked two single rooms for the night, Reg had his first appearance at the university the next day. After some sight-seeing we both had a kip, got showered and went to the dining-room for dinner, we were both tired out and retired to our rooms for 10 p.m. I crashed out and fell into a deep sleep.

When I awoke the next morning I was surprised to find Reg sat in the armchair in my room! He had a big grin all over his face.

'What's tickling you?' I queried.

"I've done it!' he said excitedly, 'I've traveled to the future, only ten minutes mind, but into the future nonetheless.'

'Brilliant!' I exclaimed, 'And with no side effects this time.'

'I can prove it, for in exactly five minutes time the bellboy will knock on the door of your room and ask if you want anything.'

I looked at my watch, it was exactly 9 a.m. Sure enough at 9:05 a.m. there was a knock at the door, it was the waiter, I opened the door: 'Do you need anything Sir, like a newspaper or coffee?'

'I would like coffee for two,' I said absentmindly.

When the waiter had gone I slapped Reg on the back and said, 'You did it, you son of a gun you've traveled in time!'

After lunch we both prepared for the short trip to the university for Reg's first lecture in the United States. When we got there I sat in the audience—Reg's style of delivery soon had everyone interested in what he had to say, he had the ability to charm and beguile his audience and make everything perfectly clear, except when it came to the mathematics. Now that was a different story—Reg had had to create his own equations to fit the theory and this is where understanding was left high and dry—no one knew what the hell he was on about. But the math had to be correct otherwise we wouldn't be able to roam the universe like we did.

We spent the evening in the local bar where Reg had his followers and admirers who gathered around him asking all sorts of questions, I noted with satisfaction that no-one asked about matter transference and time travel.

Next stop—Washington was more of the same, we spent some of the time sightseeing and then Reg's lecture. It was here that Reg decided he would travel to the past, we were both in my room at about ten at night. One minute Reg was standing there and then POP! He was gone. No sooner had he gone than he was back again.

'What happened Reg, did it work?' I enquired.

'Sure did. I traveled a day into the past, I know it was yesterday because all the newspapers were carrying the date.'

'Can you touch anything in the past?' I queried.

'No, because that would cause fluctuations in the space time continuum. What happens in the past affects the future. And what happens in the future cannot be influenced by the appearance of matter in that dimension.'

'So it's not the same, even though we transfer matter it is still in the present, so we can affect that dimension,' replied Reg.

'When can I travel in time, Reg?'

'Leave it for the time being,' he replied.

I wondered why Reg was holding out on me, he usually couldn't wait to share his latest discoveries with me. I couldn't help showing my disappointment and I could see he'd noticed it.

We traveled on through America visiting all the sights with Reg holding his lectures and seminars in the various cities of the USA. Soon we arrived at San Francisco which was the last venue of Reg's tour. We were in the bar in a downtown area of the city on the last night, when we were approached by two young lovelies who said they were astrophysicists. They were telling the truth because they showed a knowledge in physics that was above and beyond the norm. The drinks kept coming and soon Reg was getting the worst for wear. One of the girls soon had her arm around his neck and was looking adoringly into his eyes.

'I bet you two would love to know the true con . . . con . . . conclusion of my theory wouldn't cha,' slurred Reg.

I looked up in alarm, Reg was close to spilling the beans about his theory! (Luckily I wasn't as plastered as Reg.)

'Come on, it's time for bye byes,' I said staring fixedly at Reg.

'No, not yet, it's . . . it's early yet, and besides these two would love to know about my theory, es . . . es . . . especially the one with the baby blue eyes!'

One of the girls said, 'Just let us go to the bathroom and then you can tell us everything.' She patted Reg on the cheek. With that they both got up and went to the loo.

'Come on Reg, it really is time for your bed, we have a plane to catch tomorrow.' I said in desperation, 'You don't want them to know the true meaning of your theory do you?'

Just then I noticed a flash of lucidity in Reg's eyes.

'No, no, I guess not.'

'Well, come on then, get up,' I muttered, tugging at his arm and pulling him to his feet.

I slung his arm around my neck and steered him to the exit, out of the corner of my eye I could see the two girls coming back to where we had been seated.

'D . . . d . . . do you know Dick, I don't know what I'd do without you,' said Reg through an alcoholic mist. Outside I managed, somehow, to hail a taxi.

I got Reg to his room and tucked him up in bed, fully clothed, well, I wasn't going to undress him was I?

The next morning Reg was well and truly hung over, I ordered black coffee to be sent up to the room.

'What happened last night?' he asked, 'All I can remember is meeting those fit young girls who said they were astrophysicists.'

'Well you were that close to telling them the true nature of your theory,' I said holding my thumb and forefinger together in front of his face.

'Blimey I must have been pissed,' he retorted.

A few cups of coffee and a couple of aspirin later and Reg was somewhere near normal. I thought about the two young girls, they couldn't have been foreign agents, could they?

I drove us both to the airport after we had packed, Reg had earned himself a cool 12 grand on the tour. The plane was dead on time and as we flew home I realised how much I had missed Prue and my daughters. Reg was pining for Marcia and his son, too. After the plane had landed I got us a taxi for Reg's house where I had left my car. Marcia was outside in the garden when we pulled up and ran down the path and flung herself into Reg's arms. 'Oooh, I've missed you,' she said, squeezing him tightly.

'Well I'll be off then,' I said, getting into the car.

'I'll be in contact,' said Reg, 'and thanks for everything.'

'Honestly you two, you're as thick as thieves,' said Marcia, grinning.

When I got home, Prue was waiting for me and gave me a big kiss as I entered the bungalow, 'How did it go?' she asked.

'As quick as a flash,' I said, 'It's great to be home.' I eased myself into my favourite armchair after pouring myself—yes, you've got it—a large whiskey and tonic. Coming up was a world tour starting in Paris, that would last for a month at least, I thought. Well, that was for the future, I now had to answer the barrage of questions from Prue about America.

Meanwhile, Reg was flitting from present to past to future. He was careful not to get stuck again and the furthest he went was 30 years into the future and 20 years into the past where he observed himself as he was then, a bone idle unemployed nobody drinking himself into oblivion living in his tatty terraced house. Reg was very careful not to disturb the continuum of the space time dimension he was visiting, he didn't even swat an insect and he tried not to tread where he shouldn't. He visited the past and the future very briefly so as to keep any disturbance to the minimum.

265

CHAPTER 45

I was in the garden mowing the grass when the phone rang, it was Reg, 'I've got something important to tell you Dick can you meet me in the Grey Mare in Chester today?'

'Well, yes I suppose so,' I replied, 'but what is it that's so important, can't it wait?'

'No it can't,' he said emphatically. 'I need to see you as soon as possible.'

"OK, I'll meet you in about an hour and a half's time.' He rang off. I was concerned that something was wrong with Reg's family or Reg himself, he sounded pretty serious on the phone.

'I've got to go out and see Reg,' I shouted to Prue, who was in the kitchen.

'All right, but don't be late, I'm doing spag bol for tea,' she answered.

It took me about an hour and twenty minutes to pull up in the Grey Mare's car park. When I got to the bar Reg wasn't there yet so I ordered a shandy and waited. About five minutes went by and Reg entered the bar looking as if he had the weight of the world on his shoulders. He greeted me and I ordered another shandy for him. We went into the public lounge and sat down.

'What's up with you,' I queried, 'You look like you've seen your backside.'

'Oh, God I wish that it was all,' he replied.

'Well, come on then, spill,' I said.

'Well,' said Reg taking a deep breath, 'Yesterday I traveled thirty years into the future, and oh my God, Dick the World was in turmoil.'

'What do you mean, an earthquake or something?'

'If only it were that simple,' he replied gloomily. 'You know that North Korea has tested nuclear weapons don't you?'

I sat up in alarm. 'Yes I do.'

'To cut a long story short they developed a quantity of them in 2041 along with the missiles to carry them. The USA didn't like it so it told North Korea in no uncertain terms, then the incredible, irresponsible happened. The Koreans launched a nuclear strike on three major cities in America, New York, Washington and Philadelphia causing a nuclear fall-out along the east coast. The Americans launched a single missile armed with a matter/anti-matter warhead invented as a direct result of the discovery of the Higgs boson, a super atomic missile. The warhead was so powerful that it obliterated the entire North Korean landmass, the fall-out reached into South Korea and China. China took this as an act of aggression and declared war on America in June of 2041. I was too scared to go any further in time in case I witnessed a third world war.'

There was a tear in Reg's eye. 'My God, Dick what kind of world is my son and your grandchildren going to grow up in?'

I couldn't believe it at first, then I tried to take it in rationally. 'Can't we do something about it Reg,' I uttered, 'Can't we go in there and twat the whole North Korean government or something like that?'

'Naturally, I've thought of that but the Koreans would think it was an American act of aggression anyway. There has to be answer, but to alter the future in such monumental proportions doesn't bear thinking about, the disturbance in space-time would be too great. No, I think we are stuck with the future the way it is—what will be will be,' Reg replied gloomily.

We parted company, all I could think of on the way home was the absolute importance of Reg's discovery, a nuclear war, what a waste. I went into the bungalow and noticed the grandfather clock had stopped, I went over to it and wound it up. The time was 1 o'clock.